"Get down!" Leigh yelled. "Take cover."

"I'll create a diversion," Cullen said. "I'll get the shooter to focus on me."

Leigh didn't even get the chance to say no to that because Cullen rushed to the back of the shed. He kept low, but Leigh knew it wouldn't be low enough for the bullets still coming their way.

"Don't do this," Leigh said.

He didn't listen. Cullen peeled off his jacket and thrust it out from the cover. He was making himself bait.

Hurrying, she crawled to him, took hold of his leg and jerked him back down. Cullen didn't go easily.

But the shots stopped.

Suddenly, it was quiet.

"He's getting away again," Leigh murmured.

Catching the shooter was the only way to stop him from killing again. But part of her was relieved, too. If the shots stopped, then Cullen wouldn't be gunned down.

"Don't ever do anything like that again," she snapped.

Cullen looked at her. But he didn't nod. Instead, he kissed her.

SHERIFF IN THE SADDLE

———

USA TODAY Bestselling Author

DELORES FOSSEN

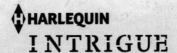

HARLEQUIN

INTRIGUE

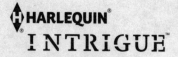

INTRIGUE™

Recycling programs
for this product may
not exist in your area.

ISBN-13: 978-1-335-58276-8

Sheriff in the Saddle

Copyright © 2022 by Delores Fossen

All rights reserved. No part of this book may be used or reproduced in
any manner whatsoever without written permission except in the case of
brief quotations embodied in critical articles and reviews.

This is a work of fiction. Names, characters, places and incidents
are either the product of the author's imagination or are used fictitiously.
Any resemblance to actual persons, living or dead, businesses,
companies, events or locales is entirely coincidental.

For questions and comments about the quality of this book,
please contact us at CustomerService@Harlequin.com.

Harlequin Enterprises ULC
22 Adelaide St. West, 41st Floor
Toronto, Ontario M5H 4E3, Canada
www.Harlequin.com

Printed in U.S.A.

Delores Fossen, a *USA TODAY* bestselling author, has written over one hundred novels, with millions of copies of her books in print worldwide. She's received a Booksellers' Best Award and an RT Reviewers' Choice Best Book Award. She was also a finalist for a prestigious RITA® Award. You can contact the author through her website at www.deloresfossen.com.

Books by Delores Fossen

Harlequin Intrigue

The Law in Lubbock County

Sheriff in the Saddle

Mercy Ridge Lawmen

Her Child to Protect
Safeguarding the Surrogate
Targeting the Deputy
Pursued by the Sheriff

Longview Ridge Ranch

Safety Breach
A Threat to His Family
Settling an Old Score
His Brand of Justice

The Lawmen of McCall Canyon

Cowboy Above the Law
Finger on the Trigger
Lawman with a Cause
Under the Cowboy's Protection

HQN

Last Ride, Texas

Spring at Saddle Run
Christmas at Colts Creek

Visit the Author Profile page at Harlequin.com.

CAST OF CHARACTERS

Cullen Brodie—The owner of the Triple R, the largest horse ranch in the county. When a woman is murdered in his home, he soon learns he's the killer's next target.

Leigh Mercer—The sheriff of Dark River, Texas, who finds herself investigating a murder tied to Cullen, her former lover. Her badge is already in jeopardy, but now so is her life.

Austin Borden—Cullen's best friend, who might know more about the murder than he's willing to say.

Kali Starling—Austin's fiancée. She also had a connection with the dead woman but claims she has no idea who killed her.

Jeb Mercer—Before this former sheriff retired, he was the law in Lubbock County, but his strained relationship with Leigh could be aiding a killer.

Deputy Rocky Callaway—He's bitter that he's not sheriff, but how far would he go to get Leigh out of office?

Bowen Brodie—Cullen's father, who has a decades-old grudge against Leigh's family.

Chapter One

There's been a murder at the Triple R Ranch.

Sheriff Leigh Mercer figured those were words no cop wanted to hear, but the dispatcher had been dead certain that was what the 911 caller had said.

Since the Triple R Ranch was in the jurisdiction of the Dark River Police Department, it was Leigh's job to check it out. But she hoped like the devil that the caller had been wrong. There hadn't been a murder in her hometown of Dark River, Texas, in nearly a decade, and for reasons other than just the obvious, Leigh wanted to keep it that way.

"You think we should call in Jeb on this?" Deputy Rocky Callaway asked her.

There was an edge to his voice, and leaning forward in the passenger's seat of the cruiser, Rocky was drumming his fingers on his holstered sidearm. The deputy was showing some nerves, and that was the only reason Leigh didn't scald him with a glance for asking that question.

Still, the question set her teeth on edge.

Jeb Mercer was her father, and before Leigh had pinned on the sheriff's badge eighteen months ago, Jeb had held that particular title for over four decades. He'd trained her. Trained Rocky, too. And even though Leigh had been duly elected after her dad's retirement, there were plenty, including Rocky, who'd always think of Jeb as the "real" sheriff.

"No, we're not bringing in Jeb," she insisted.

It was two in the morning, and she didn't need him to hold her hand at a possible crime scene. She'd already gotten Rocky out of bed since he was the deputy on call, and right now he was the only backup she intended to have.

She stepped from the cruiser, the winter wind howling and swiping at her. Mercy, it was cold, a bone-deep kind of wet cold that poked like icy fingers through her buckskin coat and boots. Leigh suspected in less than an hour, the predicted sleet would start to come down in buckets and turn the roads into skating rinks.

The wind gusts flicked away any of the usual scents that she might have picked up from the ranch, but then again, *usual* didn't apply to the Triple R. It was sprawling with its hundreds of acres of prime pastures to accommodate the hundreds of Angus cattle and prize quarter horses raised there.

The sleek white limestone house qualified as sprawling, too. Three floors that stretched out so far that it'd take a serious wide-angle lens to get it all in one photo. Lights speared out from at least a dozen of the windows.

Leigh flipped up the collar of her coat and glanced around. She hadn't been to the Triple R in fourteen years, not since she'd come to a party here when she'd been a senior in high school. She had plenty of memories of that particular event.

Memories that she hoped wouldn't get in the way if something bad had truly gone on here tonight.

Giving his own thick coat an adjustment, Rocky clamped his hand on his gun as they walked up the steps, and Leigh rang the doorbell. She automatically checked around for any signs that something was off. Nothing. And only a couple of seconds ticked by before the large double doors opened. Leigh instantly recognized the silver-haired woman who answered.

Rosa Tyree.

That was one of the advantages of living in a small town. Leigh knew most folks, and in this case, she knew that Rosa was a house-keeper at the ranch. A longtime one, having worked there for longer than Leigh had been alive. She was also well aware that Rosa didn't usually look this frazzled.

"He won't let me in the room," Rosa volunteered right away. "He said I should wait down here for you." Shivering from the cold, she frantically motioned for them to come in, and when they did, she shut the doors.

"He?" Leigh questioned though she was pretty sure she already knew what Rosa's answer would be.

"Mr. Brodie," Rosa provided, and then she added, "Mr. *Cullen* Brodie."

Yep, Leigh had been right. Cullen Brodie was the owner of the Triple R, but his brother, Nick, and their father, Bowen, visited often. Leigh had been hoping for Nick or Bowen since Cullen was a huge part of those memories that she hoped wouldn't get in the way.

"You made the 911 call?" Leigh asked the woman while she had a look around the foyer and the adjoining rooms.

Rosa nodded, followed her gaze. "The cleaning crew won't be in until morning to clear up from the party."

There was indeed some various glassware scattered on the tables in what Leigh supposed was called a great room. A room that lived up to the sprawling and plush standards of the rest of the ranch. There were also gleaming silver trays with remains of what had no doubt been tasty food. What was missing were guests, but maybe those who'd been invited to the engagement party had headed out so they could get home before the bad weather moved in.

"The, uh, body's at the back of the house," Rosa explained, fluttering her trembling fingers in that direction. "It's the big room at the end of the hall. Mr. Brodie's in there, too."

Leigh did a quick trip down memory lane and silently groaned. That was Cullen Brodie's bedroom. Or at least it had been years ago.

"Someone really got murdered here?" Rocky asked Rosa. "Who?"

"I don't know who. But that's what Mr. Brodie said, that there'd been a murder, and he told me to call 911. I didn't see the body for myself though. Please don't make me go in there," the woman quickly added. "I don't want to see a dead body."

Leigh gave her a reassuring pat on the arm. She could easily agree to Rosa's request because if this was indeed a murder, Leigh didn't want the woman anywhere on the scene.

With Rocky at her heels, Leigh made her way down the hall to the *big room*. And yep, it was big all right. The doors to the massive bedroom suite were open, and even though it'd been redecorated in the years since she'd been here, it lived up to the size in her memory.

She didn't see anything remotely resembling a dead body, but there was a live one all right. Leigh immediately spotted Cullen.

And she felt the punch of lust.

There was no other word for it. Pure, hot lust. Of course, Cullen had that effect on plenty of women, what with his rock-star face. Not a used up, has-been rock star, either, but one in his prime who could attract just by breathing. Sizzling blue eyes, midnight-black hair and a face that, well, created those punches of pure, hot lust.

He was seated in a dark red leather chair, a glass of amber liquid in his hand. The top buttons of his rumpled white shirt were undone, and his tie was tossed on the glossy mahogany table in front of him.

His gaze slid over her, settling for a long moment on the badge she had clipped to her belt. "Sheriff," he said, and there wasn't a trace of the smirk or disapproval that some folks doled out when they mentioned her title.

"Mr. Brodie," Leigh greeted in return, and it earned her a raised eyebrow from him. Probably because the only other time she'd been in this room, they'd definitely been on a first-name basis.

Since Leigh didn't want to remember that right now or think about the lust, she got down to business. "You had Rosa call 911 to report a body?"

Cullen nodded, his gesture slow and easy. The same as his movements when he got to his feet. He definitely wasn't dressed like a rancher tonight in his black pants that had no doubt been tailored for that perfect fit.

When he got closer to her, she caught his scent. And she mentally sighed. He smelled expensive.

Leigh followed Cullen to the adjoining bath, but he didn't go in. He stepped to the side to give her a clear view of the stark white room. A view that gave Leigh a gut-jab of reactions and emotions.

Sweet merciful heaven. There was blood. And lots of it. It was spattered on the tub, the walls. Even the mirror.

There was also a body.

The woman was sprawled out on the glossy white marble floor. She was a brunette with her arms and legs flailed out as if she'd tried to break her fall and then crawl away from her attacker. Maybe she'd managed to do that, but if so, she hadn't gotten far, and it hadn't helped save her. Nothing probably could have done that, considering the back of her head had been bashed in.

"Blunt force trauma," Leigh muttered, hoping if she focused on the scene and not the body that her stomach would stop churning.

She didn't normally have this kind of reaction to blood. Or a crime scene. But then, she'd never personally seen one this bad. During her time at the Lubbock Police Academy, she'd stayed on the fringes of murder investigations. An observer there to learn. Well, she wasn't an observer tonight. She was right in the thick of it.

Leigh continued to look around. Continued to study what was right in front of her. There was no weapon that she could see, and there wasn't any blood on the sharp corners of the counters to indicate that's how the woman had been fatally injured.

"Uh, you want me to call Jeb?" Rocky asked, and the shakiness in his voice had gone up some significant notches.

"No." This time Leigh didn't manage to tamp down her glare when she glanced back at him.

Along with the shakiness, Rocky looked ready to boot. She was pretty sure this was his first murder scene, too.

"Go ahead and call the medical examiner and the county CSI team," Leigh instructed. "We also need some deputies to do a room-to-room search and check the grounds. When you're done with that, take Rosa's statement. And the statements of anybody else who's in the house."

"No one else is here," Cullen provided. *Calmly* provided.

If she hadn't looked at Cullen, she might not have noticed the tight muscles in his jaw or the fierce set of his mouth. But she did look. Did notice. And she saw this had given him a gut-punch, too.

"But Jeb oughta be brought in on this," Rocky protested.

This time, Leigh didn't bother with words. She gave her deputy a look that could have frozen El Paso in August, and it was thankfully enough to get Rocky moving.

"I didn't kill her," Cullen said, those jaw muscles stirring again. "I found her when I came to my room after the party."

He didn't have to explain what party he was talking about. Small-town gossips had clued in everyone who'd listen or overhear about that. Cullen had hosted an engagement celebration for his friend Austin Borden and Austin's fiancée, Kali Starling.

According to the bits Leigh had heard, there'd been about a hundred guests, most from Lubbock, about a half hour away. Since Austin lived in Lubbock and it was where Cullen had his main office, that didn't surprise her. It was also no surprise that only a couple of locals had received invitations. Cullen hadn't exactly kept close ties with many in his hometown.

Including her.

Leigh gave Cullen another once-over, and this time she made sure the lust stayed out of it. "You wore those clothes to the party?"

Cullen nodded. "I didn't kill her," he repeated.

She believed him. Whoever had done this would have had blood spatter on him or her, and Leigh didn't see so much as a speck on Cullen. Of course, a smart killer would have changed his clothes before calling in the cops, but Leigh didn't think that was what happened here.

"It's Alexa," Cullen added when Leigh was about to go inside the bathroom.

That sent Leigh whirling back around to face him. "Alexa Daly?" she asked on a rise of breath.

Cullen nodded and had another gulp of his drink while he kept his eyes on the body.

Leigh swallowed hard. This just got a whole

lot stickier. Because Alexa was Cullen's ex-girlfriend. There'd been plenty of rumors about that, too. Leigh didn't know how much of what she'd heard about the breakup was actually true, but just about everyone agreed that it'd been a nasty one. There'd been some public arguments and rumors of a restraining order. Later, Leigh would have to suss out how much of that was gossip and how much was fact.

"Did you touch the body?" she continued, stepping inside the room. Leigh was careful to avoid any of the blood while she surveyed the area.

"Yes. I checked for a pulse on her neck. There wasn't one, and her body was already cold so I didn't try CPR. I called out for Rosa to dial 911."

So, there could be trace evidence from Cullen. She wished he hadn't made that a possibility, but it was instinct to make a check like that. Well, instinct for some. Others would have just panicked and run.

She stooped down to get a closer look at the body. Yes, it was Alexa all right, and even death hadn't been able to completely steal her beauty. Someone, however, had definitely stolen her life. Alexa's now blank emerald green eyes stared up at her.

"How many people had access to your bath-

room?" Leigh continued her examination
of the body and didn't see any self-defense
wounds. No blood or tissue under Alexa's per-
fectly manicured nails, which had been painted
bloodred.

"Anyone who came to the party, and that includes any of the catering crew who set things
up. Guests don't make a habit of coming back
here, but it does happen every now and then."

Leigh looked back at him again to see if that
was a little jab at her. After all, she had come
to his room fourteen years ago during a party.
She hadn't made a habit of doing that, either.
In fact, it'd been her first.

Cullen had been her first.

And that was yet something else that she
nudged aside.

"I'll need a guest list along with the names
of any catering staff," she told him, shifting
her focus back to the dead woman. "Include
the names of any of your ranch hands or hired
help who might have had access."

"I'll have Rosa give it to you. Alexa's name
won't be on it," he explained. "She wasn't invited, and I didn't know she was here."

Leigh wasn't surprised that Alexa hadn't
been invited, but she was wearing party
clothes. A clingy silk dress the color of expensive sapphires. Her wrists, neck and ears

glittered with gold and diamonds, which ruled out robbery as a possible motive. Well, unless the would-be thief had panicked after she'd hit the floor.

"Alexa had a key to the place?" Leigh asked.

Cullen shook his head. "I had the locks changed after we broke up, but the house wasn't locked tonight. She could have walked in except..." He paused.

"Except?" she pressed.

"She's not wearing a coat, and I didn't see one in here or in my bedroom. Plus, there's no vehicle unaccounted for in the driveway. I checked out the windows and didn't spot one," he told her. "I also don't see a purse."

"You're observant," Leigh muttered, not at all surprised by that.

The ranch was a huge success, and from all accounts, that was because of Cullen. He might not spend much time at the house, but he still ran it, and observation skills would come in handy for that.

"Did you notice anything unusual about any of your guests?" she went on.

"Do you mean did someone come into the great room with blood dripping off them?" He cursed, shook his head and seemed to gain control of that quick snap of temper. "No. It was a party. A celebration. And we celebrated."

Cullen turned away from her, groaned. "I don't know who'd do this."

"That's why I'll investigate." She paused, steeled herself up. "But you should know that I have to consider you a possible suspect."

With the same slow movements as he'd had before, Cullen eased back toward her. The breath he dragged in was long and weary. "Leigh," he said.

Just that. Only her name. But he'd made it sound like so much more. There was a plea in his tone, maybe a plea for her to believe he was innocent. And heaven help her, she did. It wasn't just the lack of blood on his clothes.

Or their very brief history together.

It was the whole package, even if that "package" was the assessment she'd been able to make so far. If Alexa and he had argued, if they'd had a fight that'd gotten out of hand, she didn't believe Cullen would have struck the woman from behind. Nor would he have removed the murder weapon only then to leave the body in place. This very well could be a crime of passion, but she didn't feel it in her gut that Cullen was responsible. Of course, she doubted anyone else was going to put much stock in her gut feeling.

Cullen scrubbed his hand over his face.

"Will what happened between us get in the way here?"

Since she'd asked herself the same thing, Leigh didn't blister him with a look or insist that nothing would get in the way of her doing her job. She couldn't. Because, yes, their past might get in the way. It wasn't like she could go back and erase memories of her first lover. Or the tangled mess that followed.

Despite her attempts to stop them, some of those memories came now. Not a gentle blur of images but crystal clear ones of Cullen's naked body. He'd been a lot younger when they'd had sex. Just nineteen. But like the rest of him, his body had been memorable even then.

"Our past won't get in the way," she answered, hoping to reassure him, and herself, that it was true. Maybe if she said it enough, both of them would start to believe it.

Stepping around Cullen, Leigh went back into the bedroom and had another look around. No blood or signs of a struggle. It was the same for the sitting area and the adjoining office. Still, the CSIs might be able to find something.

"The bedroom door was open when you came up after the party ended?" she asked.

"Closed." Cullen moved to stand beside her and followed her gaze as it skirted around the room. "Something's missing," he said.

That got Leigh's attention. "What?"

He was already moving to the sitting area, specifically to a corner table next to a leather love seat. "A bronze horse statue. It's a replica of Lobo," he added in a murmur.

The name instantly rang a bell. In the short time that she'd been involved with Cullen, his favorite horse had been named Lobo. He had won plenty of competitions, and Leigh had heard through the grapevine that Cullen had been upset when Lobo died.

"How big was the statue?" she asked.

"About a foot high, and it was heavy." He looked back at her then, and she didn't have to ask what he was thinking. Someone had grabbed it and then used it to murder Alexa.

Leigh turned when she heard the hurried footsteps coming from the hall, and several moments later, an out-of-breath Rocky came rushing into the room. He didn't have much color in his face, and he'd drawn his weapon.

"What's wrong?" Leigh immediately asked.

Rocky's chest was heaving, and it took him a moment to speak. "On one of the side porches," he finally managed to say. "There's been another murder."

Chapter Two

Hell.

That was Cullen's first reaction, but he tamped down the string of profanity going through his head and raced up the hall with Leigh. Rocky led the way, threading them through the great room and toward the west side of the house to one of the guest suites.

Cullen saw Rosa huddled in the corner of the room. The woman had obviously followed Rocky, and her breath was gusting out, causing little white wisps of fog in the freezing room. Freezing because the glass doors leading to a patio were wide-open.

"Out there," Rocky said, pointing to the patio. The deputy didn't go closer but instead stepped to the side to make way for Leigh and Cullen. "The doors were open when I came in here so I looked out and saw him."

Leigh went straight outside, her gaze firing around the side yard before settling on the man who was in a crumpled heap on the mosaic tiles. Like with Alexa's body, there was blood. Unlike Alexa, this guy was wearing a thick coat.

"It's Jamie Wylie," Cullen blurted out the moment he got a good look at the man's face. "He's one of my ranch hands."

Cullen didn't stay put. He hurried out to Jamie even though he figured there was nothing he could do, that the man was already dead.

But Cullen soon learned he was wrong.

Jamie groaned, a weak sound of raw pain, and he moved his head from side to side.

"Call for an ambulance," Leigh shouted, taking the words right out of Cullen's mouth.

Behind them, he heard Rocky make that call, and Cullen dragged the comforter off the bed. With all the blood Jamie had already lost, it was a miracle that he was still alive, but he wouldn't stay that way if he froze.

Leigh caught onto the side of the comforter and helped Cullen cover the man. "I don't want to move him," she explained. Then she threw Rocky a quick glance over her shoulder. "Tell the EMTs to hurry."

Cullen understood the urgency. There was no way to know just how serious Jamie's injuries were, and moving him inside could end up killing him. Of course, a killer could do that, too, and that's why Cullen glanced around to make sure they weren't about to be ambushed.

Beside him, Leigh was doing the same thing.

Unfortunately, this particular part of the yard had a lot of shrubs and trees that stayed thick even in the winter. It'd been landscaped that way to create a little garden oasis for guests. Which meant there were plenty of places and shadows where someone could hide. There were no views of the front or back yards, but Cullen knew there were flagstone stepping-stones that led in both directions. Alexa's killer could have gone in either direction.

Or neither.

Whoever was responsible for Jamie and Alexa could still be on the grounds. Definitely not a settling thought.

"Rosa, find one of the portable heaters and bring it out here," Cullen told the woman.

It would maybe pull her out of the shock along with helping to keep Jamie warm until the EMTs arrived, and Cullen knew there were several of the heaters in the storage room just off the kitchen. They used them for taking the chill off the patio and porches during late-night parties.

Cullen went back into the bedroom and grabbed the spare quilt and pillows from a cedar chest at the foot of the bed, and he brought those out to Jamie, too.

"It's blunt force trauma," Cullen said, looking down at the wound. Except this wasn't to the back of the head like Alexa but rather to the man's left temple. Along with the blood, there was already a huge, ugly bruise forming on his face.

Leigh nodded. She didn't touch Jamie but did lean in so that her face was right over his. "Can you hear me, Jamie? Can you tell me who did this to you?"

Jamie managed a hoarse moan. Nothing more. His eyes stayed shut, but Cullen prayed the man would be able to answer that question soon.

"Are these patio doors usually locked?" Leigh asked, aiming that question at Cullen.

"Usually, but I had a cleaning crew in the house earlier, and they could have left them unlocked."

He'd barely gotten out that answer when Leigh fired off another question. "Any idea what Jamie would have been doing out here?"

Cullen had to shake his head. "He wasn't on duty." But then he paused. "He knew Alexa."

"Knew?" Leigh pressed, and he heard the cop's inflection of what she meant.

"Nothing sexual as far as I know," Cullen

explained. "But Jamie gave her riding lessons here at the ranch."

And Cullen's mind began to play with that connection. Had Jamie brought Alexa here tonight? Cullen could see her being able to talk Jamie into doing something like that.

Maybe.

Jamie wasn't exactly a soft touch, but he was young. Barely twenty-one. And Cullen was pretty sure Jamie had been somewhat dazzled by Cullen's former girlfriend. Then again, Alexa could do lots of dazzling until you got beneath the surface and saw, well, a woman who could be obsessive and vindictive. Still, that didn't explain why Alexa was dead or why Jamie was lying there, clinging to life.

Rocky moved out onto the patio, peering down at his boss and the ranch hand. "Whoever did this musta killed the woman in the bathroom," the deputy concluded—which, of course, was stating the obvious. It was also obvious when Rocky turned an accusing gaze on Cullen.

The deputy thought he'd done this.

He doled out one of his hardest glares to Rocky, and Cullen knew for a fact that he was good at it. However, he didn't get a chance to add anything to the expression he knew would intimidate. That's because something caught Cullen's eye.

One of the small shrubs that rimmed the patio had been trampled down. He went closer, and while he didn't see any footprints, it appeared that someone had stepped on it. Maybe the someone who'd attacked Alexa and Jamie.

Leigh stood and moved closer to him, her gaze following what Cullen had spotted. "Rocky, get some photos of this with your phone. Once the EMTs arrive, they'll come rushing back here and might destroy possible evidence. Make sure you don't step on any prints."

The deputy followed her instructions just as Rosa came hurrying to the doorway. She didn't come onto the patio and didn't look at Jamie, but she did plug in the heater that she then set out on the tiles. She also handed Cullen a coat. He certainly hadn't forgotten about how cold it was, but he hadn't wanted to go inside, not with Jamie out here.

Leigh's phone rang, and because Cullen was right there next to her, he saw the name that popped up on the screen. Jeb. And he found it interesting that she hadn't listed him in her contacts as Dad but rather by his first name.

Frowning, she took the call but stepped away from Cullen. However, she continued to volley her attention between Jamie and Rocky, who was already snapping some pictures.

Cullen watched her take the cop attitude up another level and wondered if she even knew she was doing it. Probably not. It might be her go-to response when dealing with her dad. He hadn't had to hear rumors to know there was tension between Jeb and Leigh. Or at least there had been fourteen years ago when Jeb had convinced her to cut Cullen out of her life. It obviously hadn't been that hard for her to do, either, since she'd made the break and hadn't looked back.

But Cullen had.

There were times, like now, when he wondered if he should have pressed Leigh for something more. Even if that *something more* would have put even greater strain on her relationship with her father.

"Rocky shouldn't have called you," Leigh replied in response to whatever her father had just said to her. She smoothed her hand over the top of her dark brown hair that she'd pulled back into a sleek ponytail. The gesture seemed to be a way of steadying herself or maybe giving her fingers something to do other than tighten and clench. "I can handle this."

There was a long pause where Leigh was no doubt listening to Jeb's *advice*. Something that a lot of people did. Many folks still thought of Jeb Mercer as the voice of authority.

The law in Lubbock County.

It didn't matter that Jeb had been the sheriff of Dark River, a small town within the county. His lawman's reputation was legendary throughout this part of Texas.

Cullen just thought of him as a hard-nosed, bitter man who'd never gotten over his toddler son, Joe, being kidnapped twenty-seven years ago. Jeb had devoted a big chunk of his life to finding the boy, who'd now be a grown man if he was still alive. And Cullen wasn't the only one who thought that Jeb's search for his son had come at the expense of his daughter, Leigh, and his estranged son, Cash.

"I'm nowhere near ready to make an arrest," Leigh snapped a moment later, and it was definitely a snap. Judging from the quick glance she gave Cullen, he figured Jeb was already pressuring her to arrest anyone with the surname Brodie.

Hell. Old wounds and bad blood were definitely going to play into this.

"I have to go," Leigh insisted, and she hit the end call button. Cramming her phone in her pocket, she stooped back down beside Jamie and looked up at Cullen. "I'll have to bring you in for a formal interview. And not because

Jeb's pressuring to do that, but because it has to be done."

Cullen stared at her, and a dozen things passed between them. Memories. Heat. The past. Yeah. The old wounds were already surfacing.

In the distance, Cullen could hear the wail of the ambulance, but he kept his attention on Leigh. "A formal interview," he repeated, following that through. "Something you'll have to do with anyone who attended the party."

She nodded. "In the meantime be thinking of who'd want Alexa dead."

At least Leigh hadn't said *Other than you, who'd want her dead?* Though Cullen was certain Jeb would be trying to put that bug in her ear. But it wasn't true. Cullen hadn't wanted his ex dead.

"Before tonight, it's been weeks since I've given Alexa a thought," Cullen admitted.

"She didn't make any threats against you?" Leigh pressed. "Or say anything about someone threatening her?"

"No," Cullen could honestly answer. She'd made threats, yes. But they'd been verbal and none were recent. Of course, that was in part because Cullen no longer took calls from her and had refused to see her.

Leigh probably would have continued to

push for info if there hadn't been the sound of hurried footsteps. She immediately rose, laying her hand on her gun. Cullen did the same to the snub-nosed .38 that he always carried in a slide holster at the back waist of his pants. But it wasn't the killer who'd come to finish off Jamie. It was two more of Leigh's deputies. Vance Pickering and Dawn Farley.

Cullen recognized both of them and had even gone to school with Vance. He didn't know Dawn as well, but one of her brothers worked on the Triple R, and he did a good job. Hardly an endorsement for his cop sister's abilities, but at least Cullen hadn't heard anything bad about her.

"We've got a DB in the master bedroom at the back of the house," Leigh explained. "Dawn, I need you to go there and secure the scene until the CSIs and ME arrive."

"Rocky told me it was Alexa Daly?" Dawn said.

Leigh spared her a confirming nod before she shifted back to Rocky. "You will not contact Jeb again about this investigation." She kept her voice low, but Cullen still heard her. He heard her warning tone, too. "Understand?"

"But—" Rocky started.

"You will not contact Jeb," Leigh interrupted. "Now, go to the front porch and direct the EMTs here." Ignoring Rocky's huff, she turned to Vance. "I need you to check the grounds. We're not sure how the DB got here so take down the license plates of any vehicle you see. Jamie lives here at the ranch?" she asked.

It took Cullen a moment to realize that tacked-on question was meant for him, and he nodded. "He lives in the bunkhouse."

Leigh shifted her attention back to Vance as Dawn and Rocky left. "Then check there, too, and see if anyone knows what Jamie was doing on the patio."

Good question. The bunkhouse was a good quarter of a mile away from the main house, and Cullen couldn't think of a good reason why Jamie would be here in this particular spot. But he could think of a bad reason if the ranch hand had indeed helped Alexa. Help that maybe someone had objected to because Cullen doubted that Alexa had bashed Jamie on the head and then sneaked into his bedroom to have her own encounter with a killer. Then again, maybe that was exactly what'd happened.

Vance nodded at Leigh's order and stepped away, but not before giving Cullen the same kind of cop's eye that Rocky had. This time

Cullen didn't even bother with a glare because his own phone rang.

Since he didn't recognize the number, Cullen started not to answer, but then he realized it could be one of the ranch hands trying to contact him. Not a hand though because it was Austin.

"It's me," Austin immediately said. "I don't have my phone so the clerk here at the gas station let me borrow his."

Normally, Cullen wouldn't have minded a call from the man he considered a close friend, but it'd been less than an hour since Austin had left the party, and Cullen wasn't in the mood for a chat.

"I figured you'd be home by now," Cullen remarked, hoping to put a quick end to this conversation.

"I was heading that way, but the roads are bad so I was going slow. I nearly ran out of gas, too, so I stopped, and I overheard the clerk talking about his girlfriend getting called out to the Triple R. He said she was a CSI."

Cullen sighed and stepped back into the bedroom to deal with this call. This was the downside to living in a small town. Gossip, especially gossip about bad news, didn't stay hush-hush for long.

"Alexa's dead," Cullen said. "And no, I didn't kill her. I don't have a clue who did."

Austin cursed. "What the hell was she doing there?"

"Don't know that, either. In fact, I don't have answers to much of anything right now." Cullen watched as the EMTs hurried toward the patio to tend to Jamie. "But we might know something soon. Did you see anyone at the party who shouldn't have been there?" Cullen asked.

Austin paused, probably giving that some thought. "No. Are you telling me that someone came into your house and killed Alexa?"

"It looks that way." Cullen dragged in a long breath. "Maybe you could ask Kali if she saw anything? Kali got here early to make sure I didn't need any help so she might have noticed something off."

Austin paused again. "Yeah, I'll call her and ask."

Cullen's forehead bunched up. "She's not with you?"

"No. After she left the party, she went back to her folks' place for the night. I think she and her mom are doing some wedding stuff first thing in the morning. But I can tell you that if Kali had seen anything off, she would have said something to me about it. She was right by my side most of the night."

That was true, but most wasn't *all*. "You stepped outside for a smoke a couple of times," Cullen reminded him. "Did you see anything then?"

"Just one smoke," Austin corrected. "And I didn't see a thing that sent up any red flags."

Cullen pushed a little harder. "Were you anywhere near the guest room patio or the patio off my bedroom?"

"No." Austin's answer was firm and fast. "Is that where you think the killer was?"

"Yeah, along with being in my bedroom. Any chance you were in the hall outside my suite at any time during the night?"

Austin cursed. "This is beginning to sound like an interrogation, but no, I didn't go anywhere near that hall. No reason for it. Ditto for staying outside very long when I went out for that smoke. It was too damn cold."

"Sorry about the interrogation," Cullen said. "But these are questions Leigh will be asking you soon enough."

"Why me?" Austin cursed again. "Does she think I'm a suspect? Because if so, she's crazy. I didn't even see Alexa tonight."

Cullen sighed. "No. You're not a suspect. But right now anyone who was at the party will no doubt be considered a potential witness." Maybe even a person of interest. But Cullen kept that last part to himself. "We just need to find out who came into my house and committed a murder."

Austin stayed quiet a couple of seconds. "And we have to stop this person from coming after anyone else. I got that," Austin said on a heavy breath. "But give me some time to think about who it could be, and I'll get back to you."

"Thanks." Cullen watched as the EMTs loaded Jamie onto a gurney. Leigh was right there, giving them instructions about keeping Jamie secure, assuring them she'd be at the hospital soon.

"That's a lot of noise for just cops," Austin remarked. "That sounds like an ambulance siren to me."

"Because it is. Someone attacked one of my ranch hands. Jamie," Cullen provided.

"Jamie?" Austin questioned. "Hell, is he dead, too?"

"No." Cullen didn't add *not yet, anyway*, because he wanted to hang on to the hope that Jamie would pull through.

"Jamie's alive?" Austin made a sound of relief. "Then, he can tell you who attacked him?"

"To be determined. I have to go. I want to

be at the hospital when the doctors examine Jamie." He hoped Leigh wouldn't give him any hassles about that. Even if she did, Cullen would work his way around her.

The anger came now, shoving the shock aside and twisting his muscles into knots. Someone had come into his home and done this. Maybe had murdered and maimed to set him up. Yeah, Cullen would definitely get to the bottom of why this had happened.

"You need me there?" Austin asked, drawing Cullen's attention back to him.

"No. Bad weather's moving in, and I don't want you on the roads. But if you find out anything from Kali, let me know."

"I will," Austin assured him, "and keep me posted about Jamie. Hell, Cullen, he was just a kid."

Cullen didn't want that to eat away at him. But it did. Mercy, it did. All of this would eat away even when he found out who'd done this.

He ended the call and was about to go back on the patio with Leigh and the EMTs, who were about to move Jamie to the ambulance. But Leigh looked up, her gaze zooming past Cullen's shoulder and landing on someone behind him. Cullen turned and saw someone he definitely didn't want to deal with tonight.

His father, Bowen Brodie.

Bowen had ditched his party clothes and was wearing his usual jeans, including a rodeo buckle that gleamed out from his wide leather belt. Obviously, he'd had time to go to his house about fifteen minutes away and change before making his way back here, but then, Bowen hadn't stayed long at the party. He'd given his congrats to Austin and Kali and had then made an excuse about wanting to leave the shindig to the "young folks."

"I heard about the murder," his father said right off.

"It's the middle of the night," Cullen reminded him, and he didn't bother to take the snarl out of his tone. "Since you don't have ESP, someone must have called you."

Bowen confirmed that with a nod. "One of my assistants is dating the Dark River dispatcher. When he heard there'd been a murder at the Triple R, he called her."

Yeah, and had probably also called anyone and everyone in his contact list. Ditto for the dispatcher. This was big news.

"Normally, I would have cussed out anybody calling me at this hour, but I knew you'd have to deal with Jeb's spawn," Bowen added. "So I came straight over."

Spawn. That was a good way to start off

this visit. Cullen was a thousand percent sure that Leigh felt the same way he did about not wanting to deal with his father tonight.

To say that Bowen and Leigh's father had bad blood was like saying the Pacific Ocean had a drop or two of water in it. Cullen knew it went all the way back to the kidnapping and disappearance of Jeb's son. A kidnapping and disappearance that Jeb had always thought Bowen had played a part in.

Heck, maybe he had.

Bowen might be his father, but Cullen could see the man clear enough. Along with making a game of skirting the law, Bowen could be vindictive. And that vindictiveness went back to Jeb arresting Cullen's mother for a DUI. Cullen had been five years old, barely old enough to remember, but Bowen had made an art form of keeping the incident, and what followed, alive by talking about it with anyone who'd listen. That's because Cullen's mother had died in the jail cell. Alcohol poisoning, according to the ME, but Bowen had considered it negligent homicide on Jeb's part.

And so the cycle of bad blood had begun.

A cycle fueled by Jeb's firm belief that Bowen had gotten revenge by kidnapping Jeb's little boy. Apparently, the bad blood was about to continue if his father kept using words like *spawn* and glaring at Leigh.

"You're not going to railroad my son into taking the blame for something he didn't do," Bowen snarled, and he aimed that snarl at Leigh.

Leigh looked at the EMTs, motioned for them to leave. "I'll be at the hospital in a few minutes." With that, she turned to Bowen. "I don't make a habit of railroading, and I won't be starting now."

His father made a sound of disgust. "You're a Mercer. Railroading and murder are your specialties."

Cullen groaned and stepped between them, but Leigh obviously wasn't going to have any part of him running interference for her. She moved to Cullen's side and met his father's glare head-on.

"Someone's been murdered," Leigh stated, her voice a whole lot calmer than she probably felt. "I need to do my job."

She started to move past Bowen, but he caught onto her arm. Leigh looked at Bowen's grip, her brown cop's eyes sliding back to his father's equally flat ones.

"You'll want to let go of me," she said. Again, with a calm voice, but there was some fire in her expression.

"I will, when you hear me out. You're not going to pin a murder on my son because Cullen didn't kill anyone." Bowen's hand slid off Leigh's arm. "But I can tell you who did."

Chapter Three

Leigh had intended to walk away from Bowen and his 24-7 bad attitude, but what the man said stopped her in her tracks.

"You know who killed Alexa?" Leigh demanded, her narrowed gaze drilling into Cullen's father.

Bowen huffed, maybe because of her tone, maybe because of her glare. Then again, Bowen never had a positive reaction to her so he was often huffing and glaring around her.

"You need help, Sheriff Mercer?" Rocky asked. The deputy had obviously come back in the house and was eyeing Bowen as if he was a threat. Maybe Rocky thought she'd need some of his "manly" muscle to handle this situation.

She didn't.

"No, thanks," Leigh assured Rocky. "I was just asking Mr. Brodie a few questions."

Rocky gave Bowen a hard stare which didn't surprise Leigh. Rocky was loyal to Jeb, which meant the Brodies were the enemy. Plenty of people in Dark River felt the same way.

"It's freezing," Bowen snarled. "Let's take this inside, and I can tell you all about the kind of woman Alexa was."

Leigh didn't want to go inside. She wanted Bowen to finish with this revelation so she could get to the hospital. Besides, what he had to say might not be a revelation at all but just some ploy to throw suspicion off Cullen. Still, Leigh couldn't totally blow off something that might help with the investigation, so with the tip of her head for Bowen to follow her, she stepped through the patio doors. Rocky didn't leave, but he did step to the side so there'd be room for Bowen and Cullen.

The guest room was quiet, but it wouldn't stay that way. It'd likely be only a matter of minutes before the ME and CSIs arrived. Too bad this second crime scene had already been compromised. Rosa, Cullen and now Bowen had already been in the room. Rosa was no longer there, but, of course, Cullen was right there next to Leigh when she turned to his father.

"Make this quick," Leigh told Bowen. "I'll do a formal interview with you in the morning, but for now I want to hear about who wanted Alexa dead."

"I don't know his name," Bowen explained. "But Alexa met with him."

When he didn't add more, Leigh made a circling motion with her index finger for him to continue. That gesture earned her another huff.

"I hired a PI to follow Alexa," Bowen blurted out, his gaze shifting to Cullen. "She was threatening you, and I wanted to make sure she didn't do anything stupid."

Leigh volleyed glances at the two men, and she saw the surprise on Cullen's face, the steely resolve on Bowen's. Bowen clearly didn't think he'd done anything wrong by trying to micromanage his son's life.

"I wanted to make sure she didn't do anything stupid," Bowen repeated, the resolve also in his voice. "I didn't want Alexa to try to smear your name. Or worse. Have her try to do something violent. Hell hath no fury like a woman scorned," he added.

Leigh wasn't sure Alexa had actually been scorned, but she wanted to hear more. "I take it this PI found out something about her?"

Bowen nodded, kept his unapologetic eyes on his son. "Yesterday, Alexa had a meeting with a man in a café in Lubbock. The PI said the guy was carrying concealed, that he saw the bulge from a shoulder holster beneath his coat."

"Maybe he had a license to carry concealed," Leigh pointed out when Bowen paused again.

"Maybe," Bowen agreed. "But when the PI took a table near them, he heard Alexa and this man mention Cullen. Specifically, Alexa said she wanted the man to deal with Cullen."

"Deal with?" Leigh and Cullen repeated in unison.

"Yeah, and I don't have specific details of what she meant by that. The PI said that Alexa and this man quit talking when someone else took a table nearby, and they went outside to finish their conversation. The PI wasn't able to hear anything else they said."

Leigh looked at Cullen to see what his take on this was, but he only shook his head. "You believe Alexa was hiring this man to do something to me?" Cullen asked his father.

"Yes, I do. I think that's obvious. She wanted this guy to hurt or kill you."

Well, it wasn't obvious to Leigh. Possible, yes. But not absolute proof of the woman's guilt. Still, Alexa was dead so this could very well be connected.

"I'll want the name of your PI," Leigh insisted.

"Thought you would." Bowen extracted a business card from his coat pocket and handed it to her.

Leigh glanced at the card only to note the PI's name, Tyson Saylor. She'd be calling him very soon.

"This should be enough for you to back off Cullen," Bowen went on. "Alexa probably had her hired goon bring her here tonight. So she could witness him killing or hurting Cullen. Then, I'm guessing something went wrong. Maybe the goon wanted more money, and when Alexa wouldn't pony up, he killed her."

Obviously, Bowen had given this some thought, but it was still just a theory. One that might not have any proof to back it up.

"I'll investigate this—" Leigh assured him.

"And you'll lay off Cullen," Bowen interrupted. "Don't you think about arresting him because of what's gone on between our families."

Leigh heard the weariness in her own sigh. "At the moment I have no plans to arrest Cullen or anyone else for that matter because there's no clear-cut evidence to point to who did this."

Bowen released the breath he appeared to have been holding, and he gave a crisp nod before turning back to Cullen. "Call me if you need anything."

So, she'd apparently appeased Bowen enough for him to get out of her face. Not

Rocky though. Her deputy was aiming a questioning look at her. Probably because he believed there was indeed some *evidence to point to who did this*.

And Rocky no doubt thought the pointing should be at Cullen.

"Check with Dawn and make sure both crime scenes are secure," she instructed Rocky, not only to remind him that she was the sheriff and was therefore in charge but also because it was something that needed to be done. "I'm going to the hospital to get an update on Jamie." With some luck, she might even be able to question the ranch hand.

"I could go with you," Rocky suggested.

"I need you here," she insisted, and Leigh motioned for Cullen to follow her toward the front door. "Depending on how long I'm at the hospital or Jamie's condition, I might be able to get your statement in the next hour or two. I suspect you'll want a lawyer there for that."

Cullen had already opened his mouth, but he seemed to change his mind as to what he'd been about to say. "I'm going to the hospital, too. Jamie works for me," he added in a snap before she could protest.

She saw the weariness on his face. The worry. Not for his own situation but for Jamie. And that's why Leigh didn't tell him to stay put. Even though that would have been the smart thing to do. It'd keep Cullen out of her hair while she gathered evidence. Then again, it would keep him away from the crime scene, too. Cullen would no doubt be able to handle any flak that Rocky tried to dole out to him, but this would hopefully keep Rocky focused on his assigned duties so he wouldn't be able to take jabs at Cullen.

"You can ride in the cruiser with me," she offered, "but you'd have to find your own way back here once we're done at the hospital and my office."

Cullen didn't object to that, so Leigh reached for the knob on the front door. However, before she could open it, Vance called out to her.

"Wait up," the deputy said, hurrying through the great room toward them. "I think I found the murder weapon." He took out his phone, showing her a picture. "I didn't touch it. Figured I'd leave it where it is for the crime scene guys to collect."

It was a bronze horse statue of Lobo.

"Where'd you find that?" Cullen demanded.

Vance waited until he got a nod from Leigh before he answered. "In some bushes on the patio off the master bedroom. I'm guessing the killer went out through the patio doors and tossed it there."

That put a knot in Leigh's stomach. Because anyone wanting to pin this on Cullen would point out that the weapon had been in Cullen's bedroom and that Cullen would be the one to most likely have access to it.

But Cullen wasn't stupid.

Only a stupid killer would have tossed the murder weapon so that it could be easily found. That meant it probably didn't have anything on it that could be linked back to who'd used it to bash in Alexa's head. Then again, maybe the killer had tossed it out of panic. Or because he or she had been in a hurry. Either way, this was going to put some pressure on her to arrest Cullen.

"If the CSIs aren't here before the sleet starts, hold an umbrella over the statue so we don't lose any prints or trace," Leigh told Vance. "Once it's been bagged and tagged, mark it priority and have a courier take it to the lab."

Vance nodded, and as Rocky had done, he gave an uneasy glance at Cullen. "You heading somewhere?"

"Cullen and I are going to the hospital."

Vance's uneasiness seemed to go up a notch. "You okay with that?"

She heard the deputy's underlying concern.

That maybe she was about to get in the cruiser with a killer. It didn't sting as much coming from Vance as it had with Rocky. That's because Vance didn't have the fierce loyalty to Jeb that Rocky did. Or the equally fierce hatred of the Brodies.

"I'm okay," she assured Vance. "Call me if you find anything else. I need to know how Alexa got here tonight. And don't forget to question the other ranch hands in the bunkhouse about Jamie. We need to find out how he ended up on the patio. Rocky can help you with that."

Leigh stepped outside and could have sworn the temp had dropped even more. Worse, she heard the first pings of ice start to hit against the porch. She hoped that Vance would get the statue protected in time and considered going back in to make sure that happened. But her best bet at getting to the truth wasn't a statue that had likely been planted to frame Cullen. Her best bet was to question Jamie.

"Before you say anything," Leigh told Cullen as they headed down the steps. "I'm going to Mirandize you."

Cullen didn't curse, but the look he shot her was colder than the sleet needling against her face.

"It's necessary," she explained. "And no, it doesn't mean I've changed my mind about your guilt. It's a way of covering my butt if you happen to say something—*anything*—connected to this murder investigation that could seemingly incriminate you."

Cullen still hadn't cursed, but Leigh belted out some mental profanity. Because this was something she should have already done.

"Do you understand your rights?" she asked when she'd finished reciting the Miranda warning.

"I understand" was all he said. Or rather grumbled. And then he got in the passenger's seat of the cruiser.

Cullen was clearly insulted and riled. It was a good thing Leigh hadn't started to weave any fantasies about having a hot night with her former lover.

Except she had.

Mercy, she had. No matter how much she tried to push away this attraction, it just kept coming back.

"Do you have enemies?" she asked, pulling the cruiser out of the driveway. Leigh headed for the road that would take them into town. "Someone who'd want to cause trouble for you?"

"Of course," he readily admitted. "I'm a

businessman, and I'm sure more than a few people thought they got the short end of the stick in a deal. But I don't know of anyone who'd set me up by murdering Alexa and bashing in the head of one of my ranch hands."

His voice and expression weren't so cold now. Oh, no. There was heat, and it wasn't from attraction. This was a storm of fury that Cullen was no doubt fighting to rein in. He looked formidable. And dangerous.

"Your father obviously hated Alexa," she pointed out.

"Yes, but Bowen didn't kill her," Cullen snapped before she could add anything else. "My father has bent the law too many times to count, but he wouldn't kill my ex-girlfriend in my bathroom and leave her body for me to find."

On the surface, she had to agree with Cullen about all of that. But maybe Alexa's murder hadn't been planned. Maybe it'd been an impulse kill. Ditto for the attack on Jamie. If so, that changed the rules. People didn't always make good decisions when panicked and trying to cover up a crime.

"Your father was at the party?" she asked. She mentally cursed again. This time when she tried to clear the sleet away with the windshield wipers, it left icy smears on the glass.

"He was." Cullen paused. "He left early. And no, he didn't seem upset or rattled. Maybe distracted," he added in a mumble. "Maybe because he knew he'd have to tell me about the PI he hired."

Maybe. That certainly had to be weighing on Bowen's mind. But it also gave the man a motive for murder. Cullen had no doubt come to the same conclusion.

"My advice," Cullen said a moment later, "have one of your deputies question my father. It'll go easier on both of you if you're not the one to do the interview."

Probably. But Leigh intended to do the questioning herself. When exactly that would happen though, she didn't know. Jamie came first, and then after she'd gotten everything she could from him, she'd need to contact the PI Bowen had hired. PIs often took pictures, and if he had, they might get an ID on the man Alexa had met in the café.

Because she had no choice, she turned on the wipers again and gave the windshield a spray of the cleaner that had a deicer in it. Her tires weren't shimmying on the road yet, but they soon would. Definitely not good because this was a narrow ranch road with deep ditches on each side.

Leigh saw the flash of lights to her left. But only a flash. She barely had time to process it when an SUV came barreling out from a cluster of trees.

And it slammed right into the cruiser.

Chapter Four

The collision happened fast. Too fast for Cullen to do anything to try to lessen the impact.

His shoulder and the side of his head rammed against the side airbag as it deployed. The seat belt snapped and caught, clamping like a vise over his chest and pinning him against the seat.

Probably with some help from the sleet, the cruiser went into a skid, and beside him, Leigh fought with the steering wheel. Trying to keep them on the road. She might have managed it, too, if the driver of the SUV hadn't come at them again. With the headlights on high beams, the SUV rammed them from behind, the front end of it colliding with the rear of the cruiser.

The impact slammed the cruiser headfirst into a tree.

There was the sound of metal tearing into the wood along with the swoosh of the front airbags when they punched into their faces. It knocked the breath out of Cullen for a couple of seconds, and the powder that'd surrounded the airbags flew into his eyes. Still, he forced himself to react, not to give in to the shock. Because he was certain of one thing.

Someone was trying to kill them.

The first impact could have possibly been an accident. Someone losing control as they came out of one of the trails. But the second collision had been intentional and with the purpose of causing them to crash into the tree. Which was exactly what'd happened.

Cullen glanced at Leigh to make sure she was conscious. She was, but she looked a little dazed. Still, she was already fumbling for her gun, which meant that she, too, had figured out that someone was using a vehicle to attack them.

The SUV came at them again.

This time the vehicle didn't just plow into them. Instead, the driver began to inch forward, sandwiching the cruiser between the SUV and the tree. Cullen had no idea if the front end of the SUV could actually crush the cruiser like an accordion, and he wasn't about to wait to find out.

Cullen batted away the airbag so he could take out his gun. It wasn't an easy task since there wasn't much room to move around. He finally managed it and soon saw that Leigh was still struggling to draw her own weapon.

"You need backup. I'm armed and stopping whoever's doing this," Cullen said, giving her a heads-up.

Leigh might have argued with him if she'd actually had her gun out and if this hadn't been a life-and-death situation where there hadn't been time to call for backup. Instead, Leigh just kept frantically shoving the airbag aside and battling to get her damaged door open while Cullen barreled out of the cruiser. He took aim at the windshield of the SUV, right where the driver would be.

Leigh finally got hold of her gun, and she must have given up on getting her door open because she climbed out through the passenger's side. The moment her feet landed on the ground, she lifted her body, and she pointed her gun at the SUV.

"I'm Sheriff Mercer," Leigh called out. "Stop or I'll fire."

Cullen wasn't surprised when the driver stopped. After all, the windshield probably wasn't bulletproof, and he or she had two guns aimed at him. Unfortunately, because of the high beams, the darkness and the heavily tinted windshield, Cullen couldn't see who was behind the wheel.

But it was almost certainly Alexa's killer.

That reminder had Cullen moving several steps closer, and he bracketed his right wrist with his left hand so his aim wouldn't be off.

On the other side of the cruiser, Leigh came forward, too, but she'd barely made it a step when the driver threw the SUV into Reverse and hit the accelerator. The tires fishtailed some, but he managed to keep control.

While he sped away.

Cursing, Cullen ran out onto the road, and he shot at the tires, hoping to disable the vehicle. He needed to see who was inside. Needed to see who was doing this so the snake could be put behind bars.

With her breath gusting and her gun still gripped in her hand, Leigh took aim at the SUV, too, but the driver had already disappeared around a curve. The road led back to the Triple R, but Cullen doubted that's where this clown was going. Not when there were many trails that the driver could use to turn. Trails that would lead back to the main road.

"I need to call this in," Leigh said in between those gusts of breath, and Cullen noticed that she was limping when she went back to the cruiser.

"Are you hurt?" he asked.

"I'm fine." It was the tone of someone who didn't want to be bothered with such questions.

Cullen didn't blame her for the attitude. Not with the adrenaline and anger pumping through them. But maybe she wouldn't put up a protest about being examined by an EMT or doctor.

Behind him, Cullen heard Leigh use the radio in the cruiser to call for backup and put out an all-points bulletin on the SUV. What she couldn't give the dispatcher was the info on the license plates. That's because they were missing, and Cullen figured that was by design. A way of making sure no one ID'd the vehicle or the driver.

Cullen stayed put on the road, and he listened and kept watch just in case the SUV returned for another round. He actually hoped that would happen, and then he could put some bullets through the windshield instead of the tires.

The wind had picked up considerably, and it was whipping the ice pellets through the air. The sleet stung his face, but he stayed put, and a few seconds later, Leigh joined him on his watch.

"Vance will be here in a couple of minutes," Leigh relayed to him. "He'll look for the SUV along the way. We might get lucky," she added.

Might fell into the slim-to-none category. Unless the driver of the SUV was a complete idiot, that is. Because anyone would have been able to figure out that Leigh would have called for backup, and even if that backup had had to come from town, it wouldn't have taken long for help to arrive.

Leigh looked back at the mangled front end of the cruiser and muttered something under her breath that he didn't catch. Cullen caught the gist of it though.

"Yeah, this is connected to Alexa and Jamie," he said.

Leigh certainly didn't argue with him. "But was I the target, or were you?" she asked.

He looked at her, their gazes connecting, and in that moment it seemed as if all the bad blood between them vanished. Nearly being killed could do that. It could tear down the walls from the past and, well, connect you. Cullen certainly felt very connected to Leigh right now. Protective, too.

And guilty.

Because he could be the reason that she'd nearly just died. Cullen didn't know the specific motive of this killer. Not yet, anyway. But he soon would. He intended to give this plenty of thought and then go after the SOB who was responsible for this hellish night.

"I doubt the SUV will be back this way," Cullen said. The sleet was coming down harder now. "We should probably wait for Vance in the cruiser."

That would not only get them out of the bitter cold, it would also give him a chance to figure out just how badly Leigh was hurt. She was still limping as they made their way back to the cruiser and slid into the back seat. Cullen got in beside her to avoid the airbag debris in the front and so he could examine Leigh. It was too dark for him to see if there was any blood on her jeans, but he used the flashlight on his phone.

Yep, there was blood all right.

"You cut your leg," he pointed out.

"More like a scrape," she corrected. "When the SUV hit my door, it pushed against my knee."

Pushed wasn't the right word. More like *bashed*. But he couldn't exactly blame her for downplaying her injury. Not when they had much bigger problems to deal with. Still, he wanted her examined.

Leigh gave the back of the driver's seat a shove, but Cullen thought the gesture was from frustration rather than trying to create more legroom. Her frustration seemed to go up a notch when her phone rang, and she saw Jeb's name on the screen. She hit the decline button.

"Your father will press you to arrest me," Cullen threw out there.

She didn't look at him but made a sound of agreement. "But this might convince him that you're not responsible for Alexa's death."

"Maybe. But he might just say I hired someone to do this so I'd look innocent," Cullen pointed out. "After all, the collision was mainly on your side of the vehicle. You stood the greatest chance of being hurt."

Leigh made a quick sound of agreement to that, too, which meant she'd likely already considered it. Then she turned her head and stared at him. "You didn't do this," she said, and then she paused. "Would your father have done it?"

Cullen tried not to be insulted that Leigh had just asked if his father was a killer. A killer who wouldn't hesitate to murder his own son.

"Not with me in the cruiser. Bowen might be bullheaded and unable to let go of the past, but he wouldn't have put me at risk." Now Cullen was the one who paused. "But perhaps this goes back to the man Alexa met in that café. Maybe he was the one behind the wheel."

Leigh didn't get a chance to give an opinion on that because the approaching headlights grabbed their attention. With their guns ready, they got out of the cruiser, watching and waiting in case this was their attacker returning.

"It's Vance," she said, releasing a breath of what was almost certainly relief.

Cullen didn't relax just yet. He had no intention of standing down until he knew for sure there wasn't another threat. But this wasn't an SUV. It was a silver Ford truck, and it pulled to a stop directly in front of them.

"Are you okay?" the deputy asked the moment he got out. It was Vance all right, and while he'd drawn his gun, he didn't aim it at Leigh or Cullen.

"Fine," Leigh answered. "Any sign of the SUV that hit us?"

"None, and like you said, I made sure to look closely at the trails that lead off the road." Vance studied the cruiser and shook his head. "Man, that looks bad. You sure you're okay?"

"I'll live," she muttered. "No thanks to the driver of the SUV." She looked at Cullen. "You have a vehicle we can use? If not—"

"I have something," Cullen assured her. One that would hopefully handle better on the icy roads than her cruiser. Since there were more than two dozen cars, trucks and four-wheel drive vehicles at the ranch, there wouldn't be any trouble accessing one right away.

Leigh grabbed her purse from the cruiser, and they got in the truck with Vance to head back to the Triple R.

"I got the horse statue secured," Vance told Leigh as he drove. He opened his mouth, probably to continue to update his boss, but then the deputy cast a wary glance at Cullen.

"It's okay," Leigh assured Vance. "Keep going. Tell me what's happening at the ranch."

The deputy gave an uncertain nod but finally continued. "I put crime scene tape around the patio and on the front door of the house and marked the area where the shrub had been trampled. There's an umbrella over the spot in case there's a print we didn't see right off."

"Good. What about Dawn and Rocky?" Leigh asked.

"Dawn's still with the body, but I told Rocky to keep on working to get statements from the ranch hands. Oh, and the CSIs are on the way, but they're having to go slow because of the weather. The roads out of Lubbock are already pretty bad."

That meant it'd be hours, maybe even days, before the CSIs were done processing his house. Cullen could go to his dad's place, but he preferred to be closer in case something broke on the investigation. He'd use either the bunkhouse or else get a room at the inn in town.

"Once you're back at the ranch, call Rocky and have him ask the hands about the SUV," Leigh instructed. "It's dark blue, has heavily tinted windows and will have some front end damage. The license plates have been removed. I don't want the driver lying in wait at the Triple R."

Cullen sure as hell didn't want that, either, and he whipped out his phone to send a text to his top hand, Mack Cuevas. He told Mack to be on the lookout for the SUV and to assist Rocky and the other deputies with whatever needed to be done.

"I'll also need the CSIs to take a look at my cruiser," Leigh continued as they approached the ranch. "There'll be paint transfer from the SUV."

Yeah, there would be, which meant the driver would likely ditch the vehicle as soon as possible. Of course, there was always the possibility that the driver would leave traces of himself inside the SUV. Traces that the lab could use to ID him.

"Rosa mentioned that a lot of the guests were taking pictures at the party," Vance went on, pulling to a stop in the driveway in front of the house. "She thought they were posting them on social media. Might be worth having a look at them and any other pictures on the guests' phones. If you want, I'll do that first chance I get."

"Yes, do that," Leigh agreed.

Cullen went back over the night, something he was certain he'd be doing until Alexa's killer was caught, and he did indeed remember lots of picture-taking going on. However, he was pretty sure he would have remembered if anything wasn't as it should be.

"This way to the garage," Cullen told Leigh when they stepped from Vance's truck.

They started in that direction but had only made it a few steps when Leigh's phone rang again. Judging from the huff she made, she expected it to be her father again. But it wasn't.

"It's the hospital," Leigh muttered, hurrying to answer it. She didn't put the call on speaker, but Cullen had no trouble hearing what the caller said.

"Sheriff, this is Dr. Denton. I figured you'd want to know that Jamie Wylie has regained consciousness."

Leigh released another of those hard breaths. "Is he okay?"

The doctor didn't jump to answer that. "I

haven't finished the exam, but I should know something soon. In the meantime, Jamie's insisting that he talk to Cullen and you right away. He says he needs to tell both of you about what went on with Alexa tonight."

Chapter Five

Leigh tried to ignore the adrenaline crash that was coursing through every inch of her body. Especially her head. She'd known it would happen, but she didn't have time to come down right now. She also didn't have time to process that someone had just tried to murder Cullen and her. She had to focus on talking to Jamie.

Because he might be able to ID a killer.

First though, Cullen and she had to get to the hospital, and that wasn't an easy task. As predicted, the roads were an icy mess and were giving even Cullen's huge truck some trouble. She felt the tires shimmy more than a couple of times, but Leigh consoled herself with the reminder that the road conditions might prevent the driver of that SUV from trying to come after them again. Or going after Jamie.

Leigh had beefed up security as best she could by arranging to have the hospital's lone security guard posted with Jamie. That wouldn't necessarily stop someone from coming in with guns blazing, but so far this particular killer hadn't used a gun. The bronze horse statue had been a weapon of opportunity. Maybe the SUV had, too, if the driver had stolen it. But if this guy got desperate to cover his tracks by eliminating Jamie, then there was no telling what he'd do. The security guard was armed, but she didn't know how he'd react in an actual crisis. There weren't many crisis tests at the Dark River Hospital.

There were other pieces of the investigation that she needed to put together, too. She had to get into Alexa's house and her workplace to see if the woman had left any clues as to who'd killed her. That meant Leigh would likely need warrants since she would have to access emails, phone records and such.

"Thinking?" Cullen asked, his question jarring her from her thoughts. "Or trying not to think?"

She considered that a moment. "Both, I guess. I need to go over the details of the investigation, but I'd rather not relive the SUV crashing into us." Leigh looked out the window, hoping that Cullen wouldn't see her shudder when she got a flash image of that crash.

"First time anyone's tried to kill you?" he asked.

"Yes." Leigh glanced at him. "You?"

"Second. A guy in a bar once drew a gun on me. He pulled the trigger, too, but it jammed."

He'd said it almost flippantly, as if it weren't a big deal, but the muscle that tightened in his jaw told her that it had indeed been big. Of course, she doubted anyone could ever get accustomed to having someone try to kill them.

Leigh motioned to the back waist of his pants. "Is that why you always carry a gun, even to a party? At least I'm guessing you had it at the party. Or maybe you holstered it afterward?"

The tightened jaw muscle relaxed into a quick smile. Not one of humor, either. "Always trying to get details that might or might not apply to the case. You're a cop to the bone, Leigh," he remarked.

"So many people would argue with that," she disagreed, and she wanted to kick herself for opening this particular can of worms.

"So many people would be wrong." Cullen smiled when she tossed him a scowl, and this time there was some humor in it. "No, I'm not saying that to get on your good side so you won't arrest me." He paused. "And yes, I always carry a weapon. Or two."

That last remark had a dangerous edge to it. Like the man himself. Leigh was attracted to that danger. To that edge. To the part of him that she thought might never fall into the "tame" category.

And that made her an idiot.

She needed an untamed, dangerous man about as much as she needed more criticism about her having the badge or living up to the lofty standards Jeb had set. Still, her body wasn't giving her a break when it came to Cullen. Hopefully though, once the adrenaline crash was done, her head would stay steady, and she would remember that he could complicate her life in the worst kind of way. There were people who were looking for a chance to oust her as sheriff, and those people would use Cullen as ammunition to get rid of her.

Leigh checked the hospital parking lot when Cullen pulled into it. He did the same, and she knew they were both looking for that SUV. Or any signs they were about to be attacked again. But the parking lot was practically empty. She considered that to be a small blessing but continued to keep watch as he parked right by the ER doors.

Another small blessing was the police department was just up the street. Less than two blocks away. Three of her eight deputies were already tied up at the Triple R, but that left one, Kerry Yancy, on duty to man the police station and back up the security guard on Jamie.

Still, Kerry could respond in just a couple of minutes if she needed help, and if things went from bad to worse, Leigh could call in the day-shift deputies. Most of them lived just a few miles from town.

Ducking their heads against the sleet and cold, Cullen and she hurried into the hospital, heading straight to the room where she saw the security guard. "Jamie's in there," the guard said.

Leigh knew him, of course. He was Harry Harbin, and when he'd been in his prime, he'd been one of her father's deputies. That explained the cool look he aimed at Cullen. And the dismissive one he gave her. She made a mental note to have Vance schedule a reserve deputy to do security detail. Guarding Jamie was critical, and Leigh didn't want any misplaced righteousness playing into this.

She knocked once on the door but didn't wait for a response before she entered, and she immediately spotted Jamie in the bed. He was indeed conscious, with his gaze zooming straight to Cullen and her.

"Thank you for coming," Jamie muttered, his voice hoarse and weak. He was hooked up to some machines and an IV.

Dr. Denton nodded a greeting to them. So did the nurse, Amber Murdock. Amber's silent greeting, however, warmed up considerably when her attention shifted to Cullen. Leigh didn't know if Amber had been one of Cullen's bedmates or if Amber was just hoping to become one. Women in Dark River generally fell into one of those two categories.

Sadly, Leigh was both.

Well, a confirmed former lover, whose body wanted the *former* label to switch to *current*. She was going to do everything in her power to disappoint her body about that.

"Is it true?" Jamie asked right off. "Is Alexa really dead?"

Leigh glanced at the doctor and the nurse, and it only took her one look to figure out the news of Alexa's death had come from Amber.

"It's true," Leigh verified. No need to hold back on the news since it was obviously already the talk of the town, and the hospital.

Tears filled Jamie's eyes. "Dead," he repeated. "She's really dead."

Leigh gauged his reaction. His grief and shock seemed genuine enough, but for all she knew Jamie had been the one to kill Alexa. Of course, that didn't explain how Jamie had then gotten hurt, and that's why she had plenty of questions lined up for him. Apparently though, Jamie had some for her as well.

"Who killed Alexa?" Jamie demanded. "How did she die?"

"I don't know who killed her," Leigh admitted. "I'm hoping you can help with that."

Jamie started to answer, but then he shifted his attention to the doctor. "Jamie insists on talking to the two of you alone," Dr. Denton explained, and clearly the doctor wasn't happy about that. "We have more tests that need to be done, and I don't want him getting agitated or upset."

Leigh didn't fault the doctor for wanting to do what was best for his patient. But she had a job to do as well. "I think Jamie will be less agitated and upset if I'm able to arrest the person who hurt him and killed Alexa. This chat is important," she added, purposely using *chat* instead of *interview*.

On a heavy breath and with a ton of obvious reluctance, Dr. Denton nodded, and with the tip of his head, he motioned for Amber to follow him. "Keep the visit short," the doctor insisted as he left with Amber.

Leigh shut the door and went closer to the bed. She didn't bother with greetings or niceties since Jamie did indeed look exhausted, and she figured she wouldn't have much time with him. "Who attacked you?"

"I don't know," Jamie muttered. Groaning

softly, he took a moment to gather his breath. "I heard footsteps, but before I could see who it was, someone bashed me on the side of the head."

Leigh wanted to curse. Cullen probably did, too. It would have put a quick end to the investigation if Jamie had been able to give them a name. And he still might be able to do that. Sometimes witnesses and victims remembered plenty of details once they were questioned, and questioning him was exactly what Leigh planned to do.

"How did Alexa die?" Jamie pressed.

"Blunt force trauma," Leigh explained. "I think once the ME has had a chance to examine her that he'll say she had a wound similar to yours. Hers was just a lot worse."

Jamie's tears returned. "I brought Alexa to the Triple R," he blurted out and looked at Cullen. "I'm so sorry. I shouldn't have done it."

"Why did you?" Cullen asked. His voice was steady, not a trace of judgment in it, but Leigh figured he wasn't pleased about one of his hands bringing his ex to a party at the ranch.

Jamie groaned, squeezed his eyes shut a moment, and he eased his head back onto the pillow. Tears continued to slide down his cheeks. "She called me right about the time the party was starting, around seven, I guess, and said she was in town and that she wanted to know if I'd give her a ride out to the ranch. She said her car was acting up and that she didn't want to risk driving it on the country road."

"You came and got her?" Leigh pressed when Jamie didn't continue.

He groaned again, nodded. "She talked me into it. I swear, I didn't know she was gonna be killed."

Cullen came closer and sat on the edge of the bed. "How'd Alexa talk you into driving her?"

Jamie's eyes met Cullen's, and a look passed between them. Leigh supposed it was a guys' understanding thing, but she figured she got it, too.

"Alexa sweet-talked you," Leigh concluded, and it had likely involved some flirting. Maybe even the hint that she'd be interested in being with Jamie in a romantic or sexual kind of way.

"At first I told her no," Jamie went on, "that I didn't think it was a good idea for her to crash the party, but she said she wouldn't be crashing. She said she just needed a quick word with you, that she wanted you to know that she was ready to move on with her life and that she wouldn't be bothering you anymore. She insisted she wouldn't make a big scene or anything and that her chat with Cullen would be private."

"And you didn't think the party would be a bad place for her to do that?" Leigh questioned.

"Yeah, I did," Jamie readily agreed. "That's why I tried to convince her to wait, to try to see Cullen another time, but she…well, she convinced me to go get her and drive her there."

Leigh reminded herself that Jamie was very young. And if Alexa was anything like her reputation, Jamie would have been putty in her hands.

"So, you picked her up and drove her to the Triple R," Leigh summed up. "What happened next?"

His forehead bunched up. "I guess it must have been about eight o'clock by then. Some guests were still arriving so she had me drop her off at the side of the house because she said she was going to slip in and have someone on the kitchen staff go and get Cullen for her. That way, she wouldn't have to go in where the party was going on." Jamie shook his head, obviously disgusted with himself. "I know all of this sounds stupid, and I shouldn't have let Alexa talk me into taking her there."

Agreed. But Leigh had to wonder if the woman had told Jamie the truth. Had she truly just wanted to talk to Cullen? Or was there a lot more to it than that? Leigh was betting it was the latter.

"You dropped Alexa off at the side of the house where you were attacked?" Cullen asked.

Jamie nodded. "The driveway is only a couple of yards behind the trees and shrubs around the patio."

It was, and Alexa would no doubt have known the particular layout. Heck, she'd maybe even stayed in that very guest room at one time or another. At least she could have stayed there when she wasn't sharing Cullen's bed, but Leigh had heard that Alexa had started visiting the Triple R before Cullen and she had gotten involved. That was definitely something Leigh needed to question Cullen about, but according to the rumor mill, Austin's fiancée, Kali, and Alexa were close friends, and Kali had brought Alexa there often.

When Jamie reached and then fumbled for the cup of water on the table next to the bed, Cullen helped him with it. Jamie took a small sip and swallowed hard before he continued.

"After I dropped off Alexa, she told me to wait for her, that she'd only be in the house about ten minutes or so and then I could drive her back into town. She was going to get a room at the inn until she could have someone take a look at her car. She said she wouldn't be driving back to her place tonight because of the bad weather moving in."

So, Alexa hadn't planned on staying at the ranch that night. Ten minutes. Not much time for a talk to try to reassure Cullen that she wasn't going to give him any more trouble.

"Were the patio doors locked?" Leigh asked Jamie.

"No." But then Jamie stopped and shook his head. "Maybe. I didn't watch when Alexa was opening the doors so she might have had a key."

Or she could have picked the lock since Cullen had already told her that he'd changed the locks after he'd ended things with Alexa. But there was a third possibility. Someone had left the doors unlocked for Alexa. Maybe the killer. Maybe someone else she'd sweet-talked on the catering crew or the household staff. The place was so big that there was no telling how long that door had been unsecured.

"Alexa went inside the house, but she didn't come out after ten minutes," Jamie went on. "I waited, but then I started to get worried about her." His mouth trembled, more tears came, and he kept his attention pinned to Cullen. "I thought she might be getting in a row with you.

I thought you two might be arguing." His voice cracked. "But now I know she was dead."

Leigh didn't have to guess that Jamie was feeling plenty guilty about that, and he began to sob. It didn't look as if it was going to be a short cry, either. Still, she had to press him on another point.

"How long did you wait outside before you were hit over the head?" Leigh asked.

"I don't know," he answered through the sob. "Maybe twenty minutes or a half hour."

Not much time for someone to kill Alexa and then go outside to attack Jamie. And that led Leigh to another problem. How had the killer known that Jamie was on the patio waiting for Alexa?

"And you're sure you didn't see who hit you?" Cullen pushed.

Jamie shook his head again. "No. I heard the footsteps, like I said, but that was it."

"Heavy or light footsteps?" Cullen continued. "Fast or slow?"

Since Leigh had been about to ask Jamie variations of those questions, she didn't object.

Jamie's forehead bunched up again. "Fast and heavy. Like someone was running at me."

So, the killer was in a hurry to take care of Jamie. Probably because he or she hadn't wanted to be seen. That made sense. After all,

Jamie was young and fit and could have probably fended off a physical attack had he gotten the chance.

But why kill Jamie at all?

Leigh figured that went back to Alexa, too.
It was possible the killer thought she'd told
Jamie the real reason she'd come to the house.
And Leigh didn't believe that real reason was
to see Cullen. Not solely, anyway. This might
indeed go back to the man she'd met with in
the café. Maybe she hadn't trusted him to do
the job if she'd actually hired him to hurt Cullen? Or maybe she'd gone there to pay him.

"My head hurts real bad now," Jamie said.
"You think you could ask the doctor to give
me some meds?"

"Sure," Leigh readily agreed. "I'll be back
later today to check on you." And to see if he
remembered anything else. "In the meantime,
there'll be a guard on your door so you'll be
safe."

Jamie gave an almost absent nod to that
along with wincing from the pain. She gave
his hand a gentle squeeze and headed for the
door.

"If you need anything, just let me know," Cullen assured Jamie, and he walked out with Leigh.

"No one other than medical staff gets near
Jamie," Leigh reminded the guard.

When she only got a grunt of acknowledgment from Harry, she repeated it and stared at him until he verbally answered. "Yes, I got that."

"I can bring out a couple of my other ranch hands to do security," Cullen suggested. Clearly, he wasn't pleased with Harry's attitude, either.

"I'll ask Vance to arrange for a reserve deputy," she said, taking out her phone.

While Leigh fired off the text, she glanced around the ER to locate the doctor. There was no sign of him, but Amber was obviously waiting for them because she moved away from the reception desk and made a beeline toward them.

"Jamie says he's in pain and needs meds," Leigh immediately relayed.

Amber nodded. "Dr. Denton will be right back and I can let him know." She shifted her attention to Cullen. "We just got a call from the Department of Transportation. The roads in and out of town are closed."

At the exact moment Amber was relaying that info, Leigh got a text giving her the same alert. She hadn't figured she'd actually make it home for hours anyway, but with the sleet projected to continue until midmorning, there was no telling when the roads would be clear enough to drive.

"I knew you'd be stuck," Amber went on,

still talking to Cullen, "so I just called the inn, and they don't have any rooms."

Leigh wasn't actually surprised by that. The inn only had four guest rooms, and anyone who'd gotten stuck because of the weather would have already snapped those up.

"I could probably find you someplace to stay here in the hospital," Amber added to Cullen.

Leigh didn't smirk, but it was obvious that Amber's *interest* in him had gotten him that particular offer. An offer that Cullen apparently wasn't going to accept.

"Thanks," he said, "but Leigh and I are going to the police station."

She was indeed heading there as planned. Not only could she get started on work, but if she had to crash for a couple of hours, there was a cot and a sofa in the break room. Though Leigh hadn't counted on sharing such cramped quarters with Cullen. But she rethought that. Neither of them would likely get any sleep anyway, and this way she could go ahead and take his official statement.

"I need to bag the clothes you're wearing," Leigh said to him as they walked away from Amber.

Cullen's mouth quivered a little. "I'm guessing it's to cover all bases and not because you want me to strip down."

She frowned. Or rather tried to do that. Leigh knew she didn't quite pull it off. "Yes, to cover the bases. I can find something at the police station for you to wear."

"I've got a change of clothes in my truck. I keep a duffel bag behind the seat."

Now she did frown. "For sleepovers with admirers like Amber," Leigh muttered, cursing herself the moment the words were out of her mouth. She so didn't need to be bringing up Cullen's sexual conquests.

"Well, actually, it has more to do with horses than admirers." That sounded very tongue-in-cheek, and he let it linger a couple of moments before he added, "I've learned the hard way to have extra clothes because I often go out to other ranches to look at horses I'm considering buying. I can get pretty sweaty, and I don't like driving back when I smell worse than the livestock."

That explanation made her silently curse herself even more. Because it gave her a giddy little punch of relief to know that he didn't make a habit of sleepovers. Then again, he could, and probably did, simply have his lovers come to his place.

Once they were outside, Leigh considered just walking to the office, but the arctic blast of air had her climbing inside Cullen's truck when he opened the door for her. He started the engine and took the time for it to warm up, which thankfully wasn't long. He pulled out of the very slippery parking lot just as Leigh's phone rang.

"It's Vance," she relayed to Cullen, and she took the call, putting it on speaker. "Guess you got the alert about the roads being closed?" she asked Vance.

"I did, and Rosa was going to call Cullen to ask if it was okay if we all stayed the night here."

"Tell Rosa that's fine," Cullen spoke up.

"Thanks, I'll tell her," Vance replied. Then, he paused. "Uh, I questioned some of the ranch hands, and I might have something."

Leigh understood the subtext in Vance's tone. She might not want Cullen to hear the *something*. But Leigh figured anything that came out of the investigation would soon make it back to Cullen's ears anyway.

"What do you have?" Leigh asked Vance.

She heard Vance take a deep breath before he answered. "Wilmer Smalley is one of the ranch hands here, and he seems reliable enough."

"He is," Cullen assured them. "Did Wilmer see someone?"

"He did," Vance verified. "He said that he

spotted two people outside the house when the party was going on. One was at the back of the house, right about where Cullen's bedroom is."

"No one should have been out there," Cullen provided before Leigh could ask him. "The catering staff would have come in through the kitchen entrance."

"Yeah, that's what Rosa said, too," Vance verified. "But he saw a man there. At least he's pretty sure it was a man, wearing a coat. He didn't get a good look at him."

"Height? Weight?" Leigh pushed.

"Wilmer couldn't say. He got just a glimpse of him before the person ducked out of sight. He said he didn't think anything of it at the time, that he figured Cullen had maybe stepped out for some reason. But he's obviously giving it plenty of thought right now."

Yes, he would be. But it helped that Wilmer hadn't immediately thought it was Cullen outside the bedroom. Even with just a glimpse, the hand should have known if it was the big boss.

"So far no one on the kitchen staff is owning up to being near Cullen's room," Vance went on. "And the kitchen entrance isn't near Cullen's room or the patio where Jamie was attacked." He paused again. "But Wilmer did see someone there."

Leigh jumped right on that. "Someone on the patio?"

"Yeah," Vance repeated. "And this time, Wilmer got a decent look at the guy's face. He says it was Cullen's good friend Austin."

"Austin?" Cullen said, the shock in his voice and on his face.

"Wilmer said he was positive that's who it was," Vance added.

Leigh immediately looked at Cullen. "Any idea what Austin would be doing out there on that particular patio?"

"None." Cullen pulled the truck to a stop in front of the police department and took out his phone. "But I'm about to find out."

Chapter Six

Cullen figured there wasn't enough caffeine in the entire state of Texas to get rid of the fog in his head. Or the headache that'd been throbbing at his temples for the past six hours. Still, he tried, and downed his umpteenth cup of coffee.

Leigh was drinking a Coke, her beverage of choice to keep her alert, but at the moment she didn't seem to be faring any better than he was. He saw her eyes droop more than once while she sat at her desk and typed away on her computer or sent texts to her deputies.

Apparently, the catnap she'd taken around 7:00 a.m. had been enough to at least keep her going, and she appeared to actually be getting work done. That included taking his official statement.

Cullen had managed some, too, in the chair next to her desk and while using a laptop that Leigh had lent him, but work was similar to coffee and his own catnap. No amount of either was going to block the images of Alexa's dead body.

Or the fact that Austin still hadn't returned his call.

Cullen had attempted the first call right after learning that Austin had been on the patio the night of the party. Something that Austin definitely hadn't mentioned in their earlier conversation. Cullen had tried three more times to get in touch with Austin, but each had gone straight to voice mail. He left another voice mail on Austin's phone at work.

It was possible the winter storm had caused some outages. Equally possible that Austin had just turned off his phone for the night and was now sleeping in. But Cullen needed to talk to his friend. So did Leigh. She'd made her own attempts to contact him, and Cullen knew those attempts would continue until she could have a conversation with him.

An official one.

Cullen didn't believe that Austin was a person of interest in Leigh's investigation, but he could tell from the terse voice mail messages she left for Austin that she suspected the man was guilty of something. Maybe the something was simply going out for a smoke. However, if Austin had used the patio for that, why hadn't he just said so? Cullen didn't know, but he just couldn't see how this connected to what had happened to Alexa and Jamie. Austin could be reckless and cocky, but he wasn't a killer.

And Cullen hoped he continued to feel that way after he heard Austin's explanation.

He doubted Leigh's deputies would give Austin the benefit of the doubt when it came to innocence or guilt. Neither would plenty of others in Dark River. Folks would want someone arrested for Alexa's murder if for no other reason than so they could feel safe in their own homes. Austin wasn't local, and worse, he had the disadvantage of being Cullen's friend. The pressure to drag Austin in and hammer away at him would grow. Well, it would once the deputies and anybody else actually managed to get into Leigh's office.

Right now, Leigh and he had the entire building to themselves since she'd sent the night deputy, Kerry Yancy, home several hours earlier. Kerry lived in an apartment just up the street so he hadn't had to drive to get there. Good thing, too, because the street glistened with ice in the morning sun, and it was too dangerous to be out driving. It would no doubt keep away any visitors—including Austin. But judging from the messages Leigh had left for Austin, she wanted him to do a phone interview and then another one with him in person as soon as the roads were clear enough for that to happen.

Leigh stood, stretched and motioned toward the break room, a location that Cullen had gotten very familiar with since it was where the coffee maker was located. "I'm going to grab a shower."

Cullen had already made use of the shower in the break room's bathroom when he'd changed into his jeans and work shirt. Thankfully, he'd had some toiletries in the bag, too, and had even managed to brush his teeth.

"There's stuff in the fridge if you want to nuke something for breakfast," Leigh added, yawning.

Her eyes met his, something that she'd been careful not to do throughout the hours they'd spent in her office. It was as if *out of sight, out of mind* was the way to go. It wasn't. And she no doubt got a full jolting reminder of that when her gaze collided with his.

She groaned, then sighed and shook her head. "I can't get involved with you," she muttered. But it sounded to Cullen as if she was trying to convince herself.

"So you've said." He let that hang in the air, and it kept hanging until Leigh mumbled something he didn't catch and walked away.

He followed her to the break room to get another refill on the coffee, and he settled down on the sofa to try to get in touch with Austin again. When he had no luck reaching him, Cullen checked the time. It was barely ten in the morning, but he was tired of waiting for Austin to return his calls so he tried Kali and cursed when she didn't answer, either.

Cullen remembered Austin saying that Kali was spending the night with her folks, but he didn't have their number so he moved on to the next call he had to make. To Mack, his ranch hand. The ever-reliable Mack answered on the first ring.

"How are things there?" Cullen asked.

"Tense," Mack said after a short pause. "The hands are nervous because the deputies have questioned them."

Cullen wished he could tell them that wouldn't continue, but it would. Each and every one of them would have to make a statement. Especially Wilmer. "Did any of the others see Austin outside during the party?"

"No. And nobody saw the other man Wilmer described, the one in the coat who he got a glimpse of by your bedroom. I'm guessing it was someone at the party who stepped out?"

"Maybe. But there were a lot of vehicles coming and going, and he could have parked somewhere and walked to that spot." He decided to go ahead and lay it out for Mack. "The guy in the coat could have been the one who killed Alexa."

"Yeah," Mack said after some thought. The word *tense* applied to him, too. Cullen could hear it in his voice.

"How's Jamie?" Mack asked.

"He's doing all right." Mostly, anyway. "He texted me after they finished running tests on him. He's got a concussion but the doctor says the signs are good that he'll make a full recovery." Dr. Denton had confirmed that when he'd called Leigh earlier.

"He's lucky," Mack concluded, and Cullen had to agree.

It'd taken nearly two dozen stitches to sew up the wound, but it could have been so much worse. If Rocky hadn't found him on the patio, Jamie might have frozen to death.

"I don't know how long it'll be before I can get back to the ranch," Cullen continued. "But keep an eye on things. And if you hear anything about the investigation, let me know."

"I can let you know that Rocky believes you're guilty," Mack readily admitted.

That came as no surprise whatsoever to Cullen. And Rocky wouldn't be the only one who thought he'd killed his ex-girlfriend. That was why it was important to Cullen that the snake who'd killed Alexa be caught. He didn't give a rat what people thought of him, but this could spill back on Leigh if enough gossips thought she wasn't doing her job by not arresting him.

Cullen ended the call with Mack and sent a text to Rosa to check and see how she was doing. He also made a mental note to give her a huge bonus for everything she was having to deal with right now. When he got a quick answer that she was okay, Cullen frowned and wished he had another text or call so he wouldn't keep thinking about Leigh.

Specifically, about a naked Leigh in the shower.

Well, at least the thought of her managed to clear out some of the cobwebs from his head. The thoughts of joining her, naked, cleared out a whole bunch more. Over the years he'd never forgotten her, but being around her like this had a way of reminding him that forgetting her was impossible.

He finally heard her turn off the water in the shower, and Cullen hoped that would quell any notion of him going in there. It didn't. Because he started to think about her dressing. Leigh had had an amazing body as a teenager, but he was betting she'd gotten even more amazing over the years.

Cullen was certain he looked guilty, and aroused, by the time Leigh came out of the bathroom. But she didn't notice, thank goodness, because she had her attention pinned to her phone.

"I got the search warrant for Alexa's home and office," she said, still focusing on the phone screen. "I'll be going through her emails, phone records, et cetera. Is there anything you'd like to tell me before I look at them?"

Cullen didn't answer right away, and he did that on purpose. He waited for Leigh to lift her gaze and look at him. "I hadn't been in touch with Alexa in months, but it's possible she kept some old emails or texts from me," he explained. "If so, there won't be any threats."

"Nothing that can be construed as a threat?" she pressed.

He gave a weary smile and went to her. "No. I don't make a habit of pouring out my heart— or my temper—in emails or texts."

She met him eye to eye. "Did you pour them out verbally?"

"Not threats. Promises," he clarified, causing her to frown.

"*Promises,*" she repeated. "Spoken like a true bad boy."

"I'm not a boy," Cullen stated. It was stupid, but he wanted to prove that to her. Prove it in an equally stupid way. And he did that by leaning in and brushing his mouth over hers.

It was too light of a touch to qualify as a kiss, but it sure as hell packed a wallop. He could have sworn that he felt it in every inch of his body.

He pulled back, gauging her reaction, and didn't think he was wrong in that she'd felt it, too. There was plenty of heat in her eyes, and it wasn't just anger that he'd done such a stupid thing.

She smelled good. Damn good. And her scent didn't have anything to do with the soap. No. This was her own underlying scent that added an extra kick to the effects of the kiss that hadn't been a real kiss.

"Leigh?" someone called out from the front of the building.

She backed away from Cullen as if he'd scalded her, and she groaned. Because it was her father's voice.

"Leigh?" Jeb called out again, and Cullen heard the man's footsteps heading their way.

Cullen didn't move, but Leigh sure as heck did. She put several feet of space between them and turned to face her father head-on when Jeb stepped through the open door. Cullen faced him, too, and he saw the instant sweep of Jeb's gaze. From Leigh to Cullen. Unless Jeb was an idiot, then he was no doubt picking up on the heated vibes in the room.

Cullen didn't see Jeb often, which he was sure both of them considered a good thing, and it'd been several years since he'd laid eyes on him. It seemed to Cullen that Jeb had aged considerably during that time. He looked older than his sixtysomething years, and being out in the cold hadn't helped his appearance. His face was chapped and red. His lips, brittle and cracked.

"The roads are closed. You shouldn't have come," Leigh insisted.

Cullen had to hand it to her. Her voice was solid, and she never once dodged her father's intense gaze.

"The county crews salted the roads about an hour ago so they should be opening back up soon. I used my big truck so I could come and check on you." Jeb paused. "I talked to Rocky, and he told me that Cullen and you had spent the night here."

Leigh nodded. "We were at the hospital when the roads were closed so we came here."

Jeb nodded, too, but it was obvious he was processing that. Along with likely trying to decide if his daughter had had sex with a man he considered a suspect.

"How's Jamie?" Jeb asked, walking past them and going to the coffeepot. He poured himself a cup and sipped while continuing to watch them.

"He's better," Leigh said just as Cullen answered, "Fine." It was Leigh who added, "But he wasn't able to ID the person who attacked him."

With just a flick of his gaze to Cullen, Jeb let her know that he was looking at the person he thought had done it. "Rocky said you'd had all the Triple R hands questioned, and—"

"I'm running the investigation by the book," Leigh interrupted. "It's all under control." Which was no doubt her way of saying her father should butt out.

Jeb didn't.

"If you were by the book," Jeb stated, his jaw tight and set, "we wouldn't be having this conversation in front of the man who should be on your suspect list."

"I didn't start this conversation," Leigh snapped. "You did when you came in here and started slinging around accusations and giving me *advice* that I don't need or want."

There was some serious temper in her tone, but it didn't last. Cullen could see that she reined herself right in. Probably because she'd had a lot of experience doing that over the years.

"Everything's under control," she repeated, much calmer this time.

She had a staring match with Jeb that lasted several long moments before Jeb huffed. "I'm worried about you," Jeb finally said, and he'd reined in most of his own temper as well. *Most.* "Someone tried to kill you."

"Someone tried to kill *us*," Leigh corrected, and she hiked her thumb toward Cullen. "We don't know which of us was the target."

Jeb opened his mouth but then closed it. He nodded, conceding that she had a point, and he downed a good bit of his coffee like medicine.

"I'm going across the street to the diner to see if Minnie needs anything," Jeb said.

Minnie Orr was the owner of the diner and someone that most folks classified as Jeb's *friend.* They were probably lovers and likely had been for years.

"Give Minnie my best," Leigh said, and she walked out of the break room, heading back in the direction of her office.

Jeb didn't follow her. Neither did Cullen, and he suspected that her father had a whole lot left to say to him. And he was right.

"You need to keep away from her," Jeb

warned him, his voice a growling whisper. "Leigh doesn't need your kind of *help*."

"She apparently doesn't need yours, either," Cullen threw back at him, and he didn't whisper. No way was he going to cover up for Jeb Mercer taking a dig at him.

Jeb flinched, finished off his coffee and slapped the cup on the table. "If you killed Alexa, I'll make sure you end up behind bars."

Cullen looked him straight in the eyes. He wasn't a cop, never had been, but he knew how to stare someone down. "Same goes for you."

Now Jeb did more than flinch. His eyes widened. "What the hell are you talking about?"

"You were a smart cop so follow the dots," Cullen spat out. "Someone killed my ex in my home. Someone who might have wanted to cause trouble for me. When I come up with possibilities of who'd want to cause that kind of trouble for me or my family, your name's always at the top of the list."

Oh, Jeb's temper returned. He aimed his index finger at Cullen, and the man's hand was shaking. "You—"

But that was all Jeb managed to say before his face went pasty white, and he staggered back a step. Since Jeb looked ready to pass out, Cullen hurried to him and caught onto his arm.

"I'm all right," Jeb insisted, and he tried to

bat Cullen's hand away, but he held on. Jeb dragged in several short breaths, wincing with each one. "You don't say a word about this to Leigh, understand?"

Cullen ignored that and went with a question of his own. "Are you sick?"

"No. I'm just a little light-headed. I need to get something to eat at the diner." Jeb finally managed to get out of Cullen's grip, and he stepped back, making eye contact with him. "Not a word about this to Leigh," he repeated.

Cullen had no intention of agreeing to that, but if Jeb was truly sick, and Cullen thought he was, then Leigh would figure it out soon enough. An illness would explain though why Jeb had decided to retire while his approval ratings had still been sky-high. Of course, Jeb hadn't hinted at any health problems, only that he was ready to turn in his badge and take some time off to pursue the search for his missing son.

"I'm not going to hurt Leigh," Cullen told him while he had the man's attention. "I care for her. I've always cared for her, and I believe we would have ended up together had it not been for Bowen and you. And for me," Cullen added. "I was young and stupid and didn't stand up to the two of you back then. But I sure as hell will stand up now."

Jeb continued to stare at him for what felt like an eternity, but the man finally nodded, turned and walked out. Cullen stood there, watching him go, and wondering what the hell was going on.

Cullen took his time going to Leigh's office just in case she wanted to have a private word with her dad. Apparently though, she hadn't, because Jeb had already left and Leigh was on the phone.

"Rocky, I don't want you leaking any more info about the investigation," she snapped. She glanced up at Cullen, who stopped in the doorway, but she continued her conversation. Or rather the dressing-down of her deputy. "Yes, leaking details to my father or anyone else. Any info that needs to be doled out will come through me. Got that?"

Cullen couldn't hear how the deputy responded, but he doubted Rocky would like having Leigh go at him like that. But Rocky deserved it. It showed disrespect, going behind her back by talking to Jeb.

Leigh stabbed the end call button and shoved her phone back in her pocket. She groaned softly, pushed some wisps of hair from her face.

"How much grief did Jeb give you after I left?" she asked.

"I gave him grief right back," Cullen settled for saying. He went closer and tapped her badge. "Do you wear that because of Jeb or in spite of him?"

Leigh shook her head, and he thought she might be annoyed with the shift in conversation. Or maybe she was just annoyed. Period. She certainly had a right to be.

"I've wanted to be a cop for as long as I can remember. Not a cop like my dad," she emphasized. "I always disapproved of punishing enemies or playing favorites when it came to justice." Leigh stopped, gave a hollow laugh. "Which is exactly what Jeb thinks I'm doing now."

Cullen studied her a moment. "No, you're not doing that. If the evidence had pointed to me killing Alexa, I'd be in a holding cell right now."

She studied him, too. Then nodded. "You would be. The badge means something to me, and if I'd been Jeb's son instead of his daughter, he would have given me his blessing about becoming sheriff. And he'd put a stop to Rocky undermining me every chance he gets." Leigh paused. "But I'm not Jeb's son."

She didn't sound bitter about that. Just resigned. And in that moment Cullen despised Jeb even more than he already had. Damn the man and his backward way of thinking. Damn him, too, for hiding whatever health problems he had from Leigh and trying to make Cullen part of that secret.

"You were elected sheriff," Cullen reminded her.

"Barely," she muttered and then quickly waved that off.

Cullen didn't wave it off though. He took hold of her chin, lifting it so their gazes met. "You were elected sheriff," he repeated. "And what you said to Jeb wasn't lip service. You *are* handling this investigation."

She turned away from him. "If I fail at this, if I don't get reelected, I'll have to move. Dark River's my home, but I'll have to move so I can get another job in law enforcement. I couldn't just go back to being a deputy. Plus, whoever beats me in the next election wouldn't want to keep me around anyway."

Cullen understood the "home" roots. He had them. Ironic, since his life was often calmer and easier when he wasn't in Dark River. It would probably be the same for Leigh, but she was as grounded here as he was.

"We have more in common than you think," he reminded her. "That's why we became lovers in the first place."

She looked back at him, the corner of her

mouth lifting into a smile. "That was hormones along with the thrill of being star-crossed lovers." Leigh made air quotes for "thrill."

No way could he pretend that the heat hadn't played into her being in his bed that night. But there was more, and Cullen was certain he wasn't the only one who'd felt it. He would have reminded her of that *more*, too, but the phone on her desk rang, and the moment was lost.

Leigh hit the answer button. The speaker function, too. "Sheriff Mercer," she said.

"Sheriff Mercer," the man repeated. "I'm Tyson Saylor."

It took Cullen a couple of seconds to remember that Saylor was the PI his father had hired to follow Alexa.

"Thank you for getting back to me," Leigh told him. "I have some questions for you."

"Well, let's hope I have the right answers," Saylor replied. "In fact, I believe I have something that's going to help with your investigation."

Chapter Seven

Leigh didn't let her hopes soar, but she truly hoped that Saylor was right and that he could help. Because heaven knew, she needed some help right now.

"As Bowen told you, he hired me to keep an eye on Alexa," Saylor continued a moment later. "He thought she might be planning on doing something to cause his son some trouble."

"And was she?" Leigh asked when she saw that was the question on Cullen's face.

"That'd be my guess, but, of course, it's all circumstantial."

Leigh sighed. "I need more than just guesses."

"I understand, and I've got a lot more than that," Saylor assured her.

She tried to manage her expectations but, mercy, that was hard, especially since none of the other evidence was falling in place just yet.

"Bowen told you that Alexa met with a man in a diner, a man who was carrying a weapon," the PI continued. "Well, it turns out that the guy is indeed a thug. I was able to ID him by asking around at the diner, and his name is James McNash."

Leigh hurried to type that into the search engine on her laptop.

"A waitress at the diner says he goes by Jimbo," Saylor explained while she typed and skimmed what popped up. "He's big, mean, and he's got a sheet for multiple assaults. He spent two years in jail on one conviction and six months on another. He's got a rep for being hired muscle."

So, a criminal with violent tendencies. That didn't mean he'd killed Alexa, but it was worth looking into. Also worth looking into why Alexa was meeting with such a man.

"What's the connection between Alexa and this Jimbo?" Leigh pressed. "How'd they know each other?"

"Don't know that, but after I did some pushing, and a little bribing, one of the waitresses finally admitted to me that Alexa and Jimbo had met more than once and that she'd overheard Alexa mention Cullen's name. The waitress also heard Alexa talk about paying

Jimbo for the job. Not *a* job," he emphasized. "*The* job."

"And you think the job might have been Cullen," Leigh concluded.

She looked at Cullen, but his expression had gone icy cold. She was betting beneath all that ice, there was the heat of temper.

"I think it's a strong possibility," Saylor agreed.

So did she. But it bothered her that the waitress had offered up so much info. Yes, there'd been payment involved, but it was a lot to tell a PI. What didn't surprise Leigh was that the waitress would remember Cullen being mentioned. It wasn't a common name, and because of his wealth and power—and yes, his looks—Cullen was somewhat of a celebrity.

"I can't get into Alexa's financials, but you might be able to trace a payment to Jimbo," Saylor suggested. "And, of course, you'll want to have a talk with him for yourself. He lives on what used to be his grandfather's farm, about ten miles from Dark River."

Leigh hoped the roads were clear enough soon because she wanted to have a chat with the man today. The sooner, the better.

"I want to go with you to see him," Cullen insisted, his voice low enough that Saylor likely hadn't heard him.

Leigh sighed because she'd known that would be his reaction. She wanted to say no, but if she did, she had no doubts, none, that Cullen would just go visit Jimbo on his own. If Alexa had indeed hired a thug to hurt or kill him, then Cullen wasn't going to back off.

"We'll discuss it later," she muttered to him, holding her hand over the receiver of the phone. Then, she could try to make Cullen see that it would hurt her investigation if he was with her when she interviewed a possible suspect.

"There's more," Saylor added, getting Leigh's attention. "Over the past month, Alexa met with two other men. I don't know the identity of one of them, and she only met with him once while I had her under surveillance. I didn't get any help from any of the waitstaff on IDing the guy. Not even when I offered money. But I'm running the photo through facial recognition, and we might get lucky."

Leigh thought about that a moment. "Did Bowen see the picture? If so, he might recognize him."

Saylor made a sound of agreement. "I sent him the pictures as an attachment to emails, but Bowen's not good at opening that sort of thing. I'll call him and tell him to have a look, that it's important."

Yes, it was. "Any chance you could send me the photos so I can show Cullen?" she asked. "He might also know who he is."

"I can do that. I don't have the pictures on my phone, and my internet's down right now, but as soon as it's up and running, I'll fire them off to you." Saylor paused. "But Cullen won't need a picture for the third man who met with Alexa. I got an ID on him from some of the background data I collected on Cullen and Alexa. It's Cullen's friend Austin Borden."

Leigh's mind did a mental stutter, and the iciness vanished from Cullen's face. "Austin?" he repeated, and this time it was plenty loud enough for Saylor to hear.

"Cullen's here with me," Leigh quickly explained to the PI. "You're sure it was Austin Borden?" she pressed.

"Positive. I'm guessing he didn't mention any of those meetings to you?"

"No," Cullen said, the surprise and confusion in his voice. *"Meetings?"* he repeated. "How many of them were there?"

"Four over the past month. They met in a café once, and the other times I trailed her going into his office."

Leigh tried to figure out why Austin would have done that, and she only came up with one possibility. Well, one possibility that didn't involve anything illegal or shady. "Maybe Alexa had business with him?" Leigh suggested.

She looked at Cullen to see if that was a possibility even though she knew it'd be a slim one. Austin was a cattle broker, and Alexa didn't seem the type to need such services. Still—

Cullen shook his head in response to her silent question, and making a frustrated groan, he scrubbed his hand over his face. He also whipped out his phone, no doubt to try to call Austin again, but Leigh lifted her hand to have him hold off on that. If Austin finally answered, she wanted the first crack at him.

"I'll get those pictures to you first chance I get," the PI added a moment later. "Good luck with your investigation, Sheriff."

The moment Leigh ended the call, she turned to Cullen. He wasn't going to like her having a go at him like this, but it had to be done. "Tell me why you think Alexa would have visited Austin," she insisted. "Were they friends?"

"Friendly," Cullen answered after a long pause. He cursed. "Hell, they were all friends. Austin, Kali and Alexa. Austin and Kali are the ones who introduced me to Alexa."

Leigh tried to jump on the "no way was Austin guilty" bandwagon, but this wasn't looking good. Especially since Austin had been spotted on the patio while the party had been going on. Added to that, the man wasn't answering his phone, and the cop in her wondered if that was because he had something to hide.

"Maybe the meetings have something to do with Austin and Kali's engagement," Cullen said several moments later. He was obviously trying to make sense of this, too. "It's possible Alexa helped him pick out the ring." He paused. "It's equally possible that Alexa was working Austin so she could figure out the best way to send a thug after me."

Of those possibilities, Leigh was choosing the last option Cullen had come up with. If it'd been something as simple as ring selection, Austin probably wouldn't have kept it from Cullen. Then again, maybe Austin felt it was best not to bring up anything to Cullen about his ex. The relationship lines became a little blurred when there was a breakup of a couple in a group of friends. Austin might not have wanted it to get around that he was staying in touch with Cullen's ex.

"All right," Leigh said, "go ahead and try to call Austin again. I've already left a message insisting he contact me immediately for questioning and then to come into the station the moment the roads are clear. If you're able to reach him, let him know I want that interview to happen ASAP."

Cullen nodded, made the call and then cursed when it went to voice mail again. She hoped Austin wasn't just trying to avoid them, but if so, she'd just pay him a personal visit after she talked with Jimbo. If he continued to dodge her, she'd be forced to get a warrant to compel him to come in for questioning.

"I'll try to call Kali again," Cullen insisted. "I can leave her another voice mail, too."

However, before he could do that, Leigh's own phone rang. She answered it and immediately heard a familiar voice.

"It's me, Jamie," the ranch hand blurted out. "Someone just threatened to kill me."

Cullen must have noticed the change in her body language and expression because he hurried to her. "Jamie," she said so that Cullen would know who was on the phone. And she put the call on speaker. "Who threatened to kill you?"

"I don't know." Jamie's voice was shaky, and she figured that shakiness applied to the rest of him, too. "I got a call from a man. It popped up on my screen as unknown, but I answered it anyway because I thought it might be somebody from the Triple R. The man's voice was muffled, but he told me if I kept talking to the cops that I'd end up like Alexa."

Sweet heaven. Leigh reined in what would have been a brusque cop tone because she knew Jamie had to be terrified. "You're still in the hospital?" she asked.

"I am, but I asked the security guard to come in the room with me. Don't tell anybody I called you. At least not until I'm out of the hospital and can fend for myself."

"I have no intention of letting you fend for yourself. The guard will stay with you and make sure you're safe. Now, tell me about this call you got." She started with an easy question. "You're sure it was a man?"

"It sure sounded like one," he answered after a pause long enough to let her know he was giving it some thought, "but like I said, his voice was muffled. You know, like someone with a bad sore throat."

The person had obviously tried to disguise his voice. Maybe because the caller had believed Jamie would recognize him.

"He threatened to kill me," Jamie repeated, and his fear had gone up another notch.

"I know. And I'm sorry. Cullen and I are just up the street. We'll be there in a few minutes and will stay with you until a deputy arrives." Leigh started putting on her coat. "I'll also need to take a look at your phone to see if we can trace the call."

"You have to trace it," Jamie insisted. "You have to stop him from killing me."

Leigh would do her best on both counts, but the trace was a long shot since the person had likely used a burner cell.

"Jamie, did Alexa ever mention someone named Jimbo McNash?" Leigh asked.

He repeated the name several times. "No. Why? Is he the man who just threatened me?"

"I don't know. But I'll find out," she promised him. "Cullen and I will be there in a couple of minutes, and we'll talk more then."

Cullen grabbed his coat, too, putting it on as they headed to the door. Leigh hated locking up, but if anyone called in with an emergency, it would go through dispatch, who would in turn notify her. She was hoping though that there wouldn't be anything else that required her attention because she already had a full plate.

"I'm texting Kerry Yancy, the night deputy, and asking him to come in," she told Cullen, and she took care of that before they went outside.

They hurried to Cullen's truck and found the windshield scabbed with ice. Since it would take precious moments to defrost it, they headed to the hospital on foot.

And they both kept watch.

Apparently, there was no need to mention to Cullen that this could be a lure to get them out into the open so that the driver of that SUV could try to kill them again. But it was a risk she had to take. Leigh wouldn't have felt right being holed up in the office while a killer went after Jamie.

"Whoever made that call could be desperate," Leigh concluded. She lowered her head against the howling wind and tried not to think of the ache that the cold air put in her lungs. "Desperate enough to try to silence Jamie, or scare him into being silenced, anyway. I need to get out the word that he didn't see anything and can't ID his attacker. In this case, the truth might keep him safe."

"I can arrange for some of the ranch hands to stand guard in the parking lot and keep an eye on who comes and goes," Cullen suggested.

Something like that would certainly cause gossip. The wrong kind of gossip, that Cullen had his nose deep in this investigation. Still, it might prevent Jamie from being hurt again.

"You trust all your ranch hands and don't

believe any one of them could have had a part in Alexa's murder?"

"I trust them," Cullen said without hesitation. "If I didn't, they wouldn't be working for me."

She considered what he said for the last block they had to walk and nodded. "Have them come out when the roads are open, but I want them to stay in the parking lot. I'll make sure security is posted inside."

And maybe none of these measures would even be necessary. It was entirely possible that the caller who'd threatened Jamie had done that as a ploy to keep the young man quiet. Thankfully, Jamie had trusted her enough to let her know about it, and Leigh wanted to make sure his trust wasn't misplaced.

They hurried into the ER, and Amber was there, waiting for them. "We've moved Jamie to another room. He was very upset so the doctor had me give him a sedative. Follow me, and I'll take you to him."

Jamie must have told Amber about the threatening call as well because the nurse was clearly shaken.

As it had been before, the hospital was still practically empty, but Leigh kept her eyes open, looking for any signs of trouble. They made their way down a hall to a room in the center of what was the patients' ward, and Cullen and she were about to go in when his phone rang.

"It's Kali," he relayed when he saw the screen. He looked at Amber when she stayed put. "I need to take this call." Cullen didn't add "in private," but Amber got the message because she strolled away, heading back to the ER.

"Kali," Cullen greeted, putting the call on speaker for Leigh. "I've been trying to get in touch with you."

"Yes." That was all Kali said for several long moments. "I got your messages, but I...well, I needed some time before I talked to you."

Oh, mercy. There was definitely something wrong, and it sounded as if the woman had been crying.

"I have to speak to Austin," Cullen continued, obviously zooming right in on what needed to be done. "Where is he?"

The next sound that Leigh heard from Kali was a sob. One that put Leigh's stomach in knots.

"What's wrong?" Cullen pressed. "What happened?"

Kali didn't answer right away. Probably because of all the crying. "I thought Austin would be with you. That's why I'm driving to Dark River now."

Cullen cursed under his breath. "Kali, it's not safe for you to be out on the roads."

"I have to see him, and he's not home. I figured he'd go to your house."

"No. If he had, someone would have called me. I'm at the hospital right now. One of my ranch hands was injured, but if Austin had shown up at the ranch, Rosa would have told me."

"Then where is he?" Kali demanded.

Apparently, Leigh wasn't the only one who wanted to know the answer to that. "I'll try to find out," Cullen tried to reassure her.

Kali didn't sound the least bit reassured though. "Did you know?" she blurted out. "Did you know about Austin?"

Because her arm was against Cullen's, Leigh felt his muscles turn to iron. "Know what?" Cullen demanded.

"That Austin was having an affair." The words rushed out, followed by another sob.

Oh, mercy. This was a new wrinkle, and Leigh already had a bad feeling about it.

"No, I didn't know about any affair. You're sure he was cheating?" Cullen pressed.

"I'm sure. I found out last night. I accidently took his phone with me."

Well, that explained why they hadn't been able to reach Austin.

"Austin's always forgetting his password so when it rang, I answered it," Kali went on. "It was just his dad wanting to make sure he got home all right after the party, but that's when I saw the texts."

"What texts?" Cullen demanded.

"God, Cullen," Kali said on a hoarse sob, "Austin's been having an affair with Alexa."

Cullen felt Kali's words land like an actual
the parents' affair

Would, I have ryy
what the I in
age her ber, w
some an lism. H
I sa the bom

Well i all i

Chapter Eight

Cullen felt Kali's words land like an actual
punch to his gut. Words that he had to mentally
repeat a couple of times just so they'd sink in.
Obviously though, Leigh wasn't having any
trouble processing what Kali had said.

"Austin had an affair with Alexa?" Leigh
asked.

"Who is that?" Kali demanded. "Who's listening?"

"Sheriff Leigh Mercer," she said.

Cullen could have told Leigh it was a mistake to volunteer who she was, and Kali's gasp
proved it. He wasn't the least bit surprised
when Kali hung up on him. On a heavy sigh,
Cullen tried to call the woman back, but Kali
didn't answer.

"For legal reasons, I had to identify myself," Leigh muttered. "And I didn't want her
to say anything incriminating that I couldn't

use because her lawyer wouldn't allow it into evidence."

Yeah, Cullen understood that, but he wished he'd been able to ask Kali if she was certain about Austin having an affair with Alexa. Then again, Leigh would almost certainly ask her when she had Kali in for questioning.

Which Leigh would do.

No way could Leigh dismiss a bombshell like that. No way could Kali dodge questioning, either, because this was a murder investigation. An investigation where Kali had just revealed a possible motive for Austin murdering Alexa. Because affairs didn't often end well. Hell, Alexa wouldn't have let it end well unless she'd been the one to call it quits.

"Let me make sure Jamie is okay," Leigh said, peering into the room. "And then we can discuss what I'm going to have to do about this situation with Austin and Alexa."

What she was going to have to do would likely include warrants. Maybe even an arrest. Yeah, this was like a punch to the gut all right.

Cullen looked in Jamie's room, too, and saw that his eyes were closed. So whatever meds Amber had given him had already taken effect. The guard, Harry Harbin, was there as well, and he actually appeared to be interested in doing his job. He was standing at the foot of the bed and had his hand on the butt of his gun.

"You need me to wake him up?" Harry asked her.

Leigh shook her head. "No. Not yet. Stay in here with him. I'll be right outside in the hall for a couple more minutes."

Harry nodded, and the moment Leigh shut the door, she turned back to Cullen. "Is Austin the type to have an affair?" she whispered. "An affair with your ex," she tacked on to her question.

"I didn't think so." Or rather Cullen didn't *want* to think so. "But obviously Kali saw something on Austin's phone to make her believe it was true. Plus, the PI said that he'd seen Alexa meet with Austin."

And there it was—the proof in a nutshell.

When he added that Austin had been spotted on the patio and that he'd kept his relationship with Alexa a secret, Cullen knew that Austin had just become Leigh's prime suspect. But Cullen could see this from one more angle.

"Even if Austin had the affair, it doesn't mean he murdered Alexa," Cullen said, thinking out loud. "But if someone found out what he was doing, they might have wanted to kill Alexa at the party to make him look guilty.

That, in turn, would sling some mud on me because some would think I'd cover for him."

Cullen was thankful when Leigh didn't ask if he would have indeed covered for his friend. He wouldn't have.

"I'm guessing Austin didn't tell you about the affair," Leigh continued a moment later, "because he…what? Would have thought you'd tell Kali?"

"I wouldn't have," Cullen insisted. "But this would have put a wedge between Austin and me. Not because he was having sex with my ex but because he was cheating on Kali. I would have tried to talk him into either ending the affair or breaking things off with Kali."

Leigh groaned softly and leaned back against the wall while she studied him. "You know this gives both Kali and Austin motive for murder. Yes, Kali said she didn't learn about the affair until she saw Austin's phone, but she could have found out sooner."

Cullen tried to imagine Kali bashing in Alexa's head, and he could see it happening if she was in a rage. But what was hard for him to fathom was that Kali would clean herself up and then come back into the party as if nothing had happened. Plus, there was the problem of Jamie. Cullen hadn't kept track of Kali's whereabouts all evening, but he just couldn't see her sneaking up on his ranch hand and trying to kill him.

Then again, people did all sorts of things to cover themselves.

And Kali might have felt the need to get rid of Jamie if she'd thought he could link her back to Alexa. Maybe Alexa had even claimed to have told Jamie that she was meeting with Kali and that if anything happened to her, Jamie would know. Again, that felt like a huge stretch.

"I need to call Mack," Cullen said, shifting his thoughts. "I want to have some extra ranch hands stand guard in the parking lot."

Leigh nodded and studied him as if she was trying to figure out just how much this latest development was eating away at him. It hurt all right, but Cullen didn't hide it from her. Wasn't sure he could.

On a sigh, she touched his arm, rubbed lightly. "I'll go in and get Jamie's phone so I can get started on the possible trace."

"Thanks for that," he said, tipping his head to the arm she'd just rubbed.

Her next sigh was louder, and despite their situation, it made him smile. This attraction was really messing with both of them.

Cullen waited until she'd gone in with Jamie

before he called Mack, and as expected, the ranch hand answered right away.

"I was about to call you," Mack said. He heard the man drag in a deep breath. "I took one of the horses over to the east trail. Just to have a look around. I wasn't far from the house when I found an SUV. There's damage to the front end so I bet it's the one used to ram into the sheriff's cruiser."

Yeah, that was a safe bet. "I'm guessing no one was inside it?"

"No one," Mack verified. "I didn't touch it, because I knew the CSIs would want to process it so I just let them know. They'll probably be calling the sheriff about it."

Again, that was a safe bet.

"It's one of the Triple R's vehicles," Mack added a moment later.

Hell. Of course it was. If the killer wanted to add another twist to muddy the waters even more than they already were, then it made sense to use one of Cullen's own SUVs. There were several on the ranch, along with a large number of trucks, and the vehicles were parked all around. There probably wouldn't have been keys in the ignition, but someone capable of killing could likely know how to hot-wire a car.

"Boss, if you're thinking one of the hands could have done this," Mack said, "you're wrong."

"I wasn't thinking along those lines. But it could have been someone who had been at the party. Someone who maybe stayed back when I thought they had left."

That would be something a killer would do—stay around to tie up any loose ends. Hell, for that matter the killer could have hidden in one of the rooms in the house. No one had done a head count to make sure all the guests had been accounted for.

And that led Cullen back to Austin.

Kali, too, since she and Austin hadn't left the party together. Plus, either one of them would have known where the SUVs were kept.

"If Austin or Kali show up at the ranch, let me know and then bring them straight in for questioning," Cullen instructed Mack. "Also, I need two more hands out to the hospital parking lot to stand guard. Jamie got a threatening phone call that shook him up."

"Will do." There was concern and some alarm in Mack's voice. "Look, I can get into town if you want me there with him."

"No, I'd rather you stay at the ranch and put out any fires that might pop up." Because after all, it was possible the killer was still nearby.

It was an unsettling thought that grew even

stronger when Cullen saw Austin coming up the hall toward him.

"I have to go," Cullen told Mack, and he ended the call so he could give Austin the once-over.

His friend looked like hell. Dark shadows under his eyes. Scruff that went well past a fashion statement, and it looked as if he'd grabbed the jeans and T-shirt he was wearing off the floor of his room. His coat was unbuttoned and flapped against his sides with his hurried strides.

"I still haven't been able to find my phone so I accessed my office messages and found all these calls from Leigh and you," Austin said right off. "What the heck's going on?"

Cullen wasn't sure where to start, and it turned out that he didn't have to make a decision about that. Leigh must have heard Austin's voice, because she came out of Jamie's room.

"What the heck's going on?" Austin repeated to Leigh.

She glanced around and motioned for him to follow her. Leigh led Austin to a small visitors' room just a few doors down from Jamie's room. Cullen went with them since he had every intention of hearing what Austin had to say. However, he waited in the doorway so he could see if someone tried to get into Jamie's room. Leigh and Austin took seats at the small metal table.

"I'm going to read you your rights," Leigh said to Austin, and she proceeded to do just that.

Austin sat in what appeared to be stunned silence before he turned his accusing gaze on Cullen. "You believe I killed Alexa?" Austin came out and demanded.

"I have questions, and I have to make sure all the legal bases are covered," Leigh insisted before Cullen could speak. "You want to call a lawyer?"

"Do I need a lawyer?" Austin fired back, but he immediately waved that off. "Let's just clear all of this up. And I can clear it up," he insisted.

The angry fire in Austin's eyes was just as much for Cullen as it was for Leigh. Cullen didn't mind. There'd be fire in his own eyes if it turned out that Austin had indeed had any part in this.

"Let's start with your whereabouts during the party," Leigh started, and she took out her phone and put on the recorder. "Were you on the patio of the guest room at the Triple R?"

Austin opened his mouth, but it seemed to Cullen that he changed his mind as to what he'd been about to say. "Yes. I was there."

"You said you smoked on the front porch," Cullen pointed out.

"Well, I misspoke." Austin stood and poured himself a cup of what looked more like sludge than coffee. It probably tasted like sludge, too, because Austin grimaced when he took a sip. "It was on the patio. It was cold, and I left the doors open so I wouldn't freeze while I was out there."

"What time was this?" Leigh said, asking the very question that Cullen knew she would.

They didn't have a time of death on Alexa, but according to Jamie, he'd dropped her off around eight. A half hour or so later, Jamie had been attacked. So, Alexa had likely died between eight and eight thirty.

"I'm not sure." Austin's forehead bunched up. "Maybe seven thirty or a little later. It was still early, but I needed a smoke before all the toasts got started so I popped outside. It was so cold that I decided to take just a few drags off the cigarette and then get a hit with the nicotine gum I carry so I wouldn't have to stay outside."

If Austin was telling the truth, then his timing for that smoke would clear him. But Leigh probably had plenty of doubts about that "if."

"Did you see anyone else on or around the patio when you were out there?" Leigh asked, and there was some skepticism not only in her voice but also in her flat cop's eyes.

"No." Austin stopped for a moment. "Well, other than a few of the ranch hands. I saw a couple of them going to and from the barn."

"Only the ranch hands?" Leigh pressed. "No one else?" When Austin shook his head, she moved on to the next question. "Did you leave the patio doors unlocked when you came back into the house?"

Again, Austin's forehead bunched up. "Maybe. Sorry, I can't remember." He huffed. "Look, I didn't kill Alexa or hurt Jamie so all of this is unnecessary."

"This is a murder investigation," Leigh argued. "All the details are necessary. Did you see Alexa during the party?" she tacked on without even pausing.

"No." However, Austin certainly did some pausing. "But she did text me. She wanted me to meet her, and I told her no."

Leigh jumped right on that. "Meet her where and why?"

Austin lifted his shoulder. "She didn't say."

"So, she could have wanted you to meet her in the house? In Cullen's bedroom?" Leigh continued.

"She didn't say," Austin repeated, and this time he snapped it. "And from the sound of these questions, I think I should call my lawyer after all."

"Go ahead." Leigh stood. "As soon as I get one of my deputies here for guard duty, I'll meet your lawyer and you at the police station. Deputy Yancy's already there and can show you to an interview room. He texted me when I was with Jamie," she let Cullen know.

Austin stood as well, and was no doubt about to verbally blast Leigh for treating him like the suspect that he was, but he didn't get the chance. Looking as harried as Austin had when he'd arrived, Kali came rushing in.

"The nurse said she saw the three of you come in here," Kali explained, her voice shaky and her glare already on Austin.

"Kali." Austin went to her and tried to pull her into his arms, but Kali batted him away and turned to Cullen. "You've told Austin that I know about his affair with Alexa?"

The color drained from Austin's face.

"No, I didn't tell him," Cullen admitted.

"Kali," Austin repeated, and again he reached for her. This time, Kali slapped him. Not a gentle hit, either. The sound of it cracked through the room.

Cullen stepped in, putting himself between the two while Leigh took hold of Austin and pulled him back.

"Don't you dare try to deny it," Kali spat out, aiming her venomous gaze on Austin. She held up what was almost certainly Austin's phone. "I found your texts to her."

It was hard for Cullen to believe this was the couple who'd been so happy just the night before. Or rather, they'd *appeared* happy. Obviously, appearances weren't accurate.

"I was going to break things off with Alexa," Austin pled. "I swear. I made a huge mistake by being with her, and I told her it was over, that I wanted to be with you. I want us to get married, Kali. I want a life with you."

The sound Kali made was a low, rumbling growl. "You'll never have a life with me."

She started cursing him, calling him vile names, but the fit of temper soon gave way to tears. Judging from her red eyes, these tears weren't the first of the day.

The sobs seemed to weaken her, and Kali sagged against Cullen. He helped her to the table and had her sit.

"I'm sorry," Austin said, but Leigh blocked him from going closer to Kali. "So sorry. You have to believe me when I tell you it was over with Alexa."

"I don't have to believe anything you say." Kali spoke through the wet sobs, and Cullen located a box of tissues for her.

"Please," Austin tried again. "Let me make this up to you."

But Kali didn't answer. She buried her face in her folded arms on the table and continued to cry.

"When did you break up with Alexa?" Cullen asked Austin, knowing that it was something Leigh also needed to know.

Austin cursed, groaned and squeezed his fists on the sides of his head. "Right before the party. She called me and said she wanted to have sex with me in your bed."

Cullen wanted to curse, too. Hell. That was something Alexa definitely would have done.

"She sent Austin a naked picture of herself," Kali provided, thrusting out the phone to Cullen.

That caused Austin to groan again, but he sure as heck didn't deny it. And Cullen could see how this had played out. Alexa had probably thought this was the way to get back at him.

Cullen took the phone from Kali and passed it to Leigh. "Did you see Alexa at any time during the party?" Leigh asked, scrolling past the naked photo to get to the texts.

"No, I swear," Austin insisted. "After she texted me, I told her I had no intentions of having sex with her in Cullen's bed or anywhere else for that matter, and I let her know that it was over. Then, I blocked her because I didn't want to have her texting or trying to call me during the party."

Leigh continued to scroll through Austin's phone. "You had this text conversation with her about the same time you said you were on the patio having a smoke," Leigh pointed out.

Austin was scowling when he whipped toward her. "I was having a smoke and texting her. You can see—I ended things with her. I ended things with her," he repeated, this time to Kali.

"I don't care," Kali snapped. "I never want to see you again."

"Unfortunately, you'll have to," Leigh said to Kali. "I'll need to interview both Austin and you. And take this into evidence," she added, holding up the phone. She looked at Austin. "Do I need a search warrant to examine the clothes you wore to the party last night, or will you give me permission to have them sent to the lab?"

Austin stared at her a long time. "You'll need a search warrant," he snarled. "Since I find myself without a phone, text Doug for me," he added to Cullen. "Tell him I'll meet him at the Dark River PD. I won't be saying anything else to Sheriff Mercer until he arrives, and I damn sure won't be giving her my clothes unless he says different."

Doug Franklin was a lawyer friend of theirs and had been at the party the night before. On a heavy sigh, Cullen sent him a text as Austin stormed out.

"I don't want to go to the police station right now," Kali muttered. "Let me just sit here for a little while and try to steady myself." She pulled off her engagement ring and practically shoved it into Cullen's hand. "Give that to him and tell him I hope he chokes on it."

"That should be fun," Cullen mumbled, slipping it into his pocket, and he stepped out into the hall with Leigh.

"I doubt they're flight risks," Leigh whispered to him, "but I want to go ahead and take Kali in after I get a deputy here to keep tabs on Jamie." She sent a text to arrange for a deputy to come to the hospital.

Cullen couldn't blame Leigh for wanting to get Kali in for questioning. The sooner they got answers, the better. Well, Cullen thought it would be better, anyway, and he hoped the woman he'd kissed less than an hour ago didn't have to arrest his friend for murder.

Leigh was no doubt trying to contain it, but the stress was starting to show, and Cullen gave her one of those arm rubs she'd given him earlier.

"That shouldn't feel good," she said, her voice still a whisper. "It can't feel good," she amended with her eyes lifting to meet his. She groaned. "This is really turning into a nasty mess."

Cullen figured he was part of that mess. A complication added to the fact that Leigh now had two suspects. Or rather three since she hadn't had a chance to talk to Jimbo Mc-Nash yet. Cullen was hoping the thug would just confess to the murder and the attacks just so the investigation wouldn't be looming over them. Then, Leigh and he could...

Well, he didn't know where they'd go from there, but one thing was for certain. He needed to figure out a way to keep her in his life. Along with getting her in his bed.

Her phone rang, and she slid Austin's cell in her jeans pocket so she could answer it and put it on speaker. "This is Saylor again," the PI greeted.

"What can I do for you?" Leigh asked.

"I got your number from Deputy Yancy when I called your office. Thought you'd want to know that Bowen had a look at the rest of the surveillance photos of Alexa, and he was able to ID the other man she met with."

Cullen leaned in so that he wouldn't miss this.

"My internet's working so I just sent the photos to you," Saylor added. "But you'll recognize the man, too."

"Oh?" Leigh asked.

"Yeah," Saylor verified. "Because it's your deputy Rocky Callaway."

Chapter Nine

The sudden shock hit Leigh to the core. "Rocky?" she managed to say to the PI. "You're sure?"

"Bowen said he's positive." Saylor paused. "He also wants to talk to you about this."

Of course he did. He'd demand to know if Rocky had conspired with Alexa to cause trouble for Cullen. Maybe for her, too. And right now, Leigh didn't have the answer to that, but she soon would.

"I photographed only one meeting that Alexa had with your deputy," Saylor continued. "But it's possible there were more."

Yes, and that was something else she would ask her deputy.

"When did this meeting with Rocky take place?" Leigh asked.

"Three days ago."

So, two days before the party. Rocky definitely should have mentioned speaking to

Alexa that close to the date of her murder. Especially since Leigh hadn't heard a peep about Rocky being friends or even friendly with the woman.

"Thanks for the info," Leigh told him, and she ended the call so she could access her email on her phone.

"I'm guessing Rocky didn't tell you about these meetings?" Cullen asked.

Leigh shook her head, pulled up the file with the photos, and the moment the first one loaded, she wanted to curse. It was Rocky all right, and she turned her phone so that he could see. Rocky and Alexa weren't exactly cozy-looking, the way lovers might be, but they were clearly having an intimate conversation.

"How bad does Rocky want to see you fail as sheriff?" Cullen asked.

Leigh suspected the answer to that was *very bad*. But she didn't voice that opinion because she spotted Cecile Taggart, a reserve deputy, heading her way. Cecile was in her early fifties and had plenty of experience. Better yet, she was someone Leigh trusted.

"I was already heading into town when I got your text," Cecile greeted. "Which one is Jamie's room?"

Leigh pointed to it. "The security guard's

with him now, but I'd rather you be in there. The guard can stay on the door."

Cecile's eyebrow winged up. "Are you expecting big trouble?"

"Trying to avoid it," Leigh explained. "Jamie's sedated right now, but he's scared. Stay with him at all times."

"Will do. I've got my laptop with me," she added, patting the bag she had hooked over her shoulder. "If you need any help with the murder investigation, just let me know. I'll probably have some downtime while I'm with Jamie."

True, especially since Jamie was asleep and might be that way for a while. "There's a search warrant to go through Alexa's files and phone records. Get started on making that happen. I need you to earmark any communication Alexa had with Austin Borden, Kali Starling and James McNash, aka Jimbo. Also with Cullen and Bowen Brodie."

Cecile's eyebrow came up again, and she glanced at Cullen, probably to see how he felt about that. Cullen merely shrugged.

"I'm covering the bases," Leigh muttered to Cullen. But, of course, she hadn't. Because she'd left Rocky's name off that list. No doubt because Leigh didn't want Rocky to know he was under investigation. And that was probably why she also added to Cecile, "Flag anything that's connected to anyone involved in this investigation. *Anyone*," Leigh emphasized.

"Will do," Cecile repeated. "You headed home to get some shut-eye?"

Leigh shook her head. "I'll be in my office."

She waited until Cecile was in with Jamie before turning back to the visitors' room. Kali was still sitting there, but she'd stopped crying. She was staring blankly at the table.

"Would you like to walk with us to my office?" Leigh asked.

Kali shook her head. "I need a few more minutes. I'll be there soon." Now she turned and looked at Leigh. "Just make sure Austin's in a room somewhere when I get there. I meant it when I said I didn't want to see him."

Leigh gave a confirming nod, and with Cullen right beside her, they started for the exit. As she walked, she pressed Rocky's number, and he answered after several rings.

"Yo," he grumbled, sounding as if she'd woken him.

"I want you at the office right now," Leigh told him.

"But the roads—"

"Are obviously clear enough since I've got two people already waiting in Interview," Leigh interrupted.

Rocky yawned. "You want me to do the interviews?"

"I want you in the office," she repeated, a snap in her voice, and ended the call.

"Are you okay?" Cullen asked her.

No, she wasn't, and Leigh made a sound that could have meant anything so that she didn't have to verify that she was far from okay. It was possible that Rocky had withheld evidence pertinent to a murder investigation. If he had, then that would be obstruction of justice.

And possibly more.

"I'm not okay," Leigh grumbled as Cullen and she walked.

"I got that. It was a tough night, followed by a tough morning."

Yes, it had been. "Thanks for not giving me any flak about having Cecile look for correspondence between Alexa and you."

"I figured you've already got enough flak. Plus, it'll be interesting to see what she kept. Like I told you, I didn't pour out my heart in emails."

She believed him. Leigh mentally groaned because it was more than just believing him. For reasons she didn't especially want to explore, she trusted Cullen, and right now, she very much needed someone who wasn't going to stab her in the back.

Deputy Yancy was at his desk when they went into the police department, and he stood, giving a nodded greeting to Cullen.

"Austin Borden's in the interview room," Yancy volunteered. "But he said he's not saying anything else until his lawyer gets here."

"I can talk to him," Cullen suggested.

But Leigh shook her head. If Austin told Cullen he was indeed a killer, she didn't want the lawyer throwing out the confession or trying to have it suppressed. Austin's lawyer could even claim that Cullen had coerced him to admit to murdering Alexa.

"When the lawyer gets here, I want you to be the one to take Austin's statement," Leigh instructed Yancy. "He's already riled at me, and you might be able to get more out of him."

Yancy was laid-back and had more of a friendly-officer style when it came to interviews. Austin might respond better to that. Heck, he might respond better to anyone other than her. Because right now, Cullen and she were the enemy.

"Dawn and Vance finished interviewing the Triple R ranch hands and the catering staff," Yancy explained. "Nothing new so far."

Leigh figured that would be the case. Still, it was a box that had to be checked.

"You know about the blue SUV being found at the ranch, right?" Yancy asked.

She nodded. "I got a text about it. Let me know when the CSIs have it processed."

"Will do. You've also got a bunch of emails and had some phone calls," Yancy added, handing her a sheet listing the calls.

"I'll get to them," Leigh said, heading into her office. "In the meantime, I need you to start securing a warrant to search Austin's home. I specifically want to get the clothes he wore to the party last night."

Yancy's eyes went a little wide. "You think there might be blood on them?"

Leigh shrugged. "We'll see when we have the clothes. Vance and Dawn might have photos from some of the guests. They were going to try to collect them. If they've managed to do that already, we'll know what clothes to include in the warrant. Unless..." She turned to Cullen. "Do you remember?"

Cullen closed his eyes a moment as if trying to call up the image. "A black suit with a blue tie. Kali was wearing a blue dress." He opened his eyes, looked at her. "I figured you'd want to know that in case you got a warrant for her clothes, too."

"I do," Leigh confirmed, giving Yancy instructions to get the warrant for that as well.

She added a search of Kali's parents' house since the woman had spent the night there. "Try to stretch the warrant to include her computer, emails and phone records." She turned back to Cullen. "And I'll have your clothes couriered to the lab this morning."

In fact, she'd already done the paperwork to get that started, and the courier would no doubt soon be on the way now that the roads were clearing. She was certain there'd be no blood on Cullen's clothes, and that might stave off those who thought he was guilty. Ironically, her own deputy Rocky was one of the ones fanning those particular "Cullen's guilty" flames, and now Leigh wanted to know if that was because Rocky had something to hide.

Because she desperately needed a caffeine hit, she went into her office to make a fresh pot. Cullen followed her, of course, and he shut the door.

"Are you going to test Rocky's clothes, too?" Cullen asked.

"If I have probable cause."

Leigh was about to continue with some legal babble to explain how she would do her job, but she cursed and gave the leg of her desk a good kick. It hurt, the pain vibrating through her boot to her toes, but she hadn't been able to hold back the frustration. No, it was more than frustration. It was a gut-punch of anger.

"Rocky will fight me every step of the way," she said on a heavy sigh. "And while he's fighting me, it'll also be a distraction from the investigation. *You're* a distraction," she added when Cullen reached for her. "You and your clothes," she grumbled.

He looked, well, amused by that, and as if she would put up no protest whatsoever—which she didn't—he pulled her into his arms and brushed a kiss on the top of her head. "My party suit or the clothes I'm wearing now?"

"The latter." She squeezed her eyes shut, and just for a moment, she let her body sag against him. "Hot cowboy clothes."

Leigh couldn't see his face, but she suspected he was smiling. After all, she'd just confessed that his well-worn jeans, faded blue work shirt and scuffed boots appealed to her more than his suit had. Then again, Cullen looked good in anything. And nothing. Especially nothing.

That, of course, only proved to her that he was a distraction.

She forced herself away from him so she could get some coffee and do some work while they waited for Rocky, Kali and Austin's lawyer. That was the plan, anyway, but the plan took a little detour when Cullen leaned in and kissed her. This was no peck like the one earlier in the break room. No. This was the full deal.

Cullen certainly hadn't lost any skills in the kissing department. He was still darn good at moving his mouth over hers. Still good at making a kiss feel as if it was full-blown foreplay. And his taste. Mercy. It was foreplay, too.

He dropped his hands to her waist, nudging her closer while also nudging her lips apart with his tongue. She remembered this. Another kick of heat. The urgency he created when he deepened the kiss.

Leigh sank into him, all the while the sane part of her yelling that she should knock this off. She listened to the sane part, knew that it was right, but she lingered a little longer, letting the kiss and Cullen's touch slide through her.

It took some willpower, but Leigh finally untangled herself from Cullen and stepped back. She didn't dodge his gaze because she needed him to see that this had to stop. Maybe she got that point across, maybe not, but either way, he didn't reach for her.

They stood there, their breaths heavy, and with the heat searing around them. She might have been tempted to go back for another round, but she was saved by the bell when her phone rang.

"It's Cash," she muttered after glancing at the name on the screen.

There was no need for her to explain that Cash was her brother, because Cullen and Cash had gone to school together. Had both been star football players. They hadn't stayed close, but then, like Cullen, Cash hadn't stayed particularly close with anyone in Dark River.

Including her.

It'd been at least six months since she'd gotten a call from him, and Leigh doubted it was a coincidence that Cash was getting in touch with her now while she was neck-deep in a murder investigation.

"Leigh," her brother greeted the moment she answered. "I just got a call from one of your deputies, Yancy. He gave me a heads-up that you'll be initiating a search warrant for Kali Starling's and her parents' residences."

Yancy worked fast, and it took Leigh several moments to realize why Cash was telling her this. Cash was the sheriff of Clay Ridge, a town about twenty miles from Dark River, and Kali and her parents lived in Clay Ridge.

"Yes," Leigh verified. "Kali was on scene at a party last night where a woman was killed."

"I heard. The dead woman was Cullen's ex.

I also heard you haven't arrested Cullen." Cash paused. "How much grief is Jeb giving you over this?"

"Enough," Leigh answered honestly, knowing it was going to cause Cash to curse.

It did.

"Damn it, Leigh, you shouldn't let him run roughshod over you like that," Cash snarled.

And there was their sibling conflict in a nutshell. After doing almost daily battle with Jeb, Cash had left home and hadn't come back. Not even for her when Leigh had insisted on staying. Cash saw that as a weakness on her part, claiming that she was Jeb's doormat. But Leigh saw it as putting up with Jeb so she could be where she wanted to be and have the job she'd always wanted.

"Jeb's never going to accept you as sheriff," Cash went on. "Not really. I mean, he might say he's okay with it, but I promise you he wanted one of his sons to take over the job."

"That's probably true," she agreed. "That's why I'm focusing on the badge. You understand that," Leigh reminded him.

Cash paused for a very long time. "Yeah. I understand." She heard him drag in a long breath. "I'll help grease the way for the warrant and will have one of my deputies execute it. What exactly do you need from Kali's place?"

"Any and all blue dresses. She wore a blue dress to the party," Leigh explained when Cash made a "huh" sound. "Also, if the warrant includes it, I want a look at her computer. Specifically, her emails. Her car is here in Dark River so one of my deputies will handle that search in case the dress is in there."

"I'll see what I can do," Cash assured her just as there was a knock on her door.

The visitor didn't wait for her to invite him in. Rocky threw open the door, his narrowed gaze spearing into Leigh.

"Thanks for everything," she told her brother. "I'll call you back later."

And she turned to Rocky.

"Cullen," she said, "could you step out while I speak with my deputy?"

Cullen moved toward the door, but Rocky stepped in front of him. "What the hell have you been telling her?" He jabbed his index finger at Leigh.

"Nothing," Leigh assured him. "But I know you've met with Alexa."

The shock widened Rocky's eyes but only for a second. Then, the anger returned with a vengeance. "Nothing," Rocky repeated, and it was coated with venom. Venom that he aimed at Cullen. "You're bad-mouthing me to Leigh because you know it should be your butt that's in jail right now."

Oh, that was not the right thing to say, and it caused Cullen to send Rocky a steely, dangerous glare. "I don't have to bad-mouth you, you idiot. You did this to yourself by meeting with Alexa."

Since Cullen was apparently going to be part of this conversation, Leigh stepped around the men and shut the door. Yancy probably wouldn't repeat anything he heard, but Leigh didn't want to air this particular dirty laundry to anyone who happened to come into the police department.

"Sit down," she ordered Rocky, and yes, she made sure it sounded like an order.

Rocky tossed out some glares of his own, both to Cullen and her, but he dropped down in the seat across from her desk.

"Before you deny meeting with Alexa," Leigh continued, "you should know that Alexa was under surveillance by a PI. He took photographs. I've personally seen the photos, and I know it's you."

Part of her hadn't wanted to give Rocky a cushion like that. A part of her had wanted him to go ahead and lie so she could reprimand him. But getting to the truth was more important than any discipline she doled out. Plus, she could dole out discipline later.

"I'm going to read you your rights," Leigh told Rocky, and she proceeded to do just that. Of course, it didn't improve his mood, and he grew angrier with each word she recited.

"You're arresting me?" Rocky spat out when she'd finished. "Good luck making any bogus charges stick."

"If I arrest you, the charges won't be bogus," she assured him. "Now, tell me why you met with Alexa, and then you can explain why you withheld this information during a murder investigation. You've been a cop long enough to know that could be considered obstruction of justice."

Rocky didn't jump to answer that, and Leigh half expected him to yell for a lawyer. But he didn't. Leigh watched as Rocky seemed to make an effort to steady himself. Maybe because he remembered that how he handled this could determine if he kept his badge. Despite his attitude, Leigh knew that wearing the badge was important to Rocky.

"Alexa called me a couple of days ago and asked if I'd see her," Rocky said. "We aren't exactly friends, but I've met her a couple of times when she's been in town with Kali.

Alexa told me that she had some questions about you."

It took Leigh a moment to realize the "you" was her and not Cullen.

"I had some business in Lubbock so I agreed to hook up with her at a diner," Rocky went on. "Alexa had heard some rumors and wanted to know if Cullen and you had started seeing each other again. I told her you weren't stupid so you wouldn't get involved with Cullen. Guess I was wrong about that," he added in a barely audible mutter.

Leigh didn't bother to blister him with a scathing look. She just motioned for him to continue.

"That was it," Rocky insisted. "Alexa just wanted to know if you two were sleeping together. When she figured out I didn't have any gossip to dish up to her, she paid for my lunch and left. And as for obstruction of justice, that's bull. I didn't obstruct squat because the meeting wasn't important. Hell, I'd forgotten all about it."

Leigh figured that last part was a huge lie. When he'd seen Alexa's dead body, it would have been logical for him to say something about the meeting he'd had with her just days earlier. Then again, maybe Rocky thought that might add him to the suspect list.

And it would have.

"Did you know that Alexa was going to the party at the Triple R?" Leigh pressed.

Rocky paused, shrugged. "She asked me about the party, wondered if me or any of the other deputies were doing security. You know, like Vance and Yancy sometimes do."

She did indeed know about that. Vance and Yancy had done some off-duty work like that when there'd been big events at the Triple R, but none of her deputies had been tapped for the engagement party.

"In hindsight, I guess Alexa asked me about that because maybe she thought I could get her into the party, but I didn't think of that until later. I didn't think of a lot of things." Rocky looked at Cullen. "I got the feeling that Alexa would do anything to get back at you."

"Well, she didn't kill herself," Leigh pointed out.

"No," Rocky quietly agreed. "But I think she was trying to stir up some kind of trouble."

"Something specific?" Cullen asked when Rocky paused.

"I'm not sure, but I figure she planned on doing something at the party. I mean, why else would she want to make sure she got in?"

If Austin was telling the truth, then Alexa had indeed planned on doing *something*, and that was getting into Cullen's bed with Austin. But Leigh figured Alexa intended to do more than just that. Maybe the woman had intended for Cullen to walk in on Austin and her.

"Why didn't you tell me about this sooner?" Leigh pressed.

"Because like I said, I'd forgotten all about it. See?" Rocky added, and some of his usual cockiness was back in his voice. "No obstruction of justice. No withholding evidence. I simply had lunch with a woman who might or might not have tried to manipulate me. Either way, I didn't have anything to do with Alexa getting into the party or being murdered, and you don't have any evidence to say otherwise."

She didn't. Leigh would give him a written reprimand for not volunteering the meeting with Alexa, but Rocky would no doubt believe it was petty. That the reprimand was because he was Jeb's ally and that he actually hadn't broken the law.

"Can I go now, *Sheriff*?" Rocky snarled, getting to his feet before she could nix that or agree. Of course, he used a mocking tone on her title. "I'm way past my normal shift hours and need some shut-eye."

Leigh nodded and watched as Rocky breezed out of her office. She battled with her temper, tamping it down—and trying not to kick the trash can again.

Rocky walked out to the dispatch desk, where Yancy was sitting, and struck up a conversation with his fellow deputy. All the while keeping an eye on Leigh. Of course, she was keeping an eye on him as well.

"Rocky could have been the one who came after us in the SUV," Cullen pointed out.

She nodded again. Heck, Rocky could have killed Alexa, hurt Jamie and then tried to kill Cullen and her—and all because he hated her and wanted her job. Then again, it was indeed possible that Rocky had done nothing wrong other than forgetting a meeting with a dead woman.

Her phone rang, and with her attention still on Rocky, Leigh pressed Answer. However, her attention wasn't on Rocky for long because the deputy gave Yancy a pat on the back and then headed out the front door.

"This is Jimbo McNash," the caller greeted Leigh. His voice was like gravel. "You left me a couple of messages, said it was real important that I call you back."

That got her attention firmly focused on the "thug" who Alexa had met at the diner. "Yes, it is important," she verified. "I have some questions for you."

"Cops," he grumbled in the same tone as Rocky had said *sheriff*. "Got a call from Cullen Brodie, too. Now, he's somebody I'd be interested in having another chat with."

Leigh didn't know that Cullen had tried to get in touch with the man, and she hit the speaker function on her phone so he could hear the rest of the conversation.

"You said Cullen Brodie called you?" she pressed.

"Yep. This morning."

Cullen shook his head. *I didn't call him*, he mouthed.

"What exactly did Cullen say to you?" Leigh asked McNash.

"He said he'd heard I'd been meeting with his woman. His ex-woman," McNash emphasized. "And he said he'd be willing to pay me to hear anything his ex told me."

"And you agreed to that?" Leigh continued.

"Sure did. So, when you come out to see me, make sure you bring Cullen and his money with you," McNash snapped right before he ended the call.

Chapter Ten

"I didn't call McNash," Cullen repeated as Leigh put her phone back in her pocket.

She nodded. "I believe you. And that means someone wanted either McNash or me to believe you'd called him."

Yeah, and Cullen had a good idea of who'd done that. "The killer or someone the killer hired."

Which, of course, didn't rule out Kali. Both Austin and she had had ample opportunity to contact McNash. Rocky had, too. But that led Cullen to another question.

"How would the killer have known about Alexa's meetings with McNash?" Cullen threw out there, but the moment the question was out of his mouth, he came up with possible answers. "Alexa told the killer. Or else McNash was the one who killed her." He paused, huffed. "Am I going to have to convince you to take me along on this visit to McNash's place?"

"No." She didn't hesitate, either. "If money's his motive, I'm counting on him telling you exactly what Alexa and he discussed. Then, if he presses you for payment, I'll arrest him for extortion." Leigh took a deep breath. "For now though, I need to find out why Kali hasn't gotten here yet."

However, Leigh didn't get a chance to do that because her phone dinged with a text.

"It's from Vance," she relayed. "The ME's finally taken Alexa's body to the morgue. We should have a verified time of death soon."

Cullen figured the TOD wasn't going to vary much from the 8:00 to 8:30 p.m. range that Jamie's timeline had already given them. Still, it was something Leigh needed to know. It was possible she'd be able to use the timeline and the photos from the guests to determine who was in the great room and who wasn't when Alexa had been murdered.

"You have Kali's number?" she asked, firing off a response to Vance's text.

Cullen took out his phone, pulled up Kali's contact, and Leigh called the woman. She put the call on speaker just as Kali answered.

"This is Sheriff Mercer. You're on your way to the police station." Leigh definitely didn't make that a question.

"No." And Cullen heard Kali sobbing again.

"I'm on my way home. I need to try to settle my nerves. I'm not running away or anything," Kali quickly added. "I just have to get myself together before you start asking me a bunch of questions."

Leigh huffed. "You should have come here."

"I know." Kali continued to sob. "But I didn't want to risk having Austin see me like this. I don't want him to know that he's crushed me. I'll be there in a couple of hours, I swear, and I'll tell you whatever I can. Promise."

Leigh's scowl deepened, and she checked the time. It was almost noon. "All right. I should be back from another interview in about three hours, and you can come in then." She paused a heartbeat. "Kali, just so you know. This interview isn't optional. If you don't show, I'll have to send a couple of my deputies over to escort you here."

"That's not necessary. I'll be there."

Leigh ended the call and glanced down at the torn knee of her jeans. And at the dried blood. It was a reminder that she hadn't gotten any medical attention. Maybe she didn't need it, but Cullen made a mental note to give her a push in that direction the next time they visited Jamie.

"I'll need to stop by my house and change my clothes," she muttered, reaching for her coat. She was still putting it on when Yancy came to the door.

"There's a problem with Austin Borden's lawyer," Yancy said. "The roads still aren't clear between here and his office in Ransom Ridge, and he can't come until later this afternoon."

"Great," Leigh muttered, and Cullen understood her frustration. Not only did she want answers from Austin, she probably also didn't want Kali and Austin squaring off when they were in the building together. "You confirmed that it's true about the roads not being clear?"

"I did," Yancy verified. "The work crews are just now salting the roads so there's still plenty of ice."

Leigh nodded. "All right. Cut Austin loose for a while. Tell him to be back here by four o'clock. Since you haven't gotten much sleep, Vance or Dawn can interview Austin and Kali. They should be back here once they're able to get away from the Triple R."

"I'm okay," Yancy assured. "I can do at least one of the interviews."

She seemed to consider that a moment and then nodded again. "All right. Make sure you do it by the book. I'm going to visit Jimbo McNash."

"I just saw that name on a preliminary report from Cecile," Yancy explained. "She sent it to you and all the deputies."

"Did Cecile see Jimbo's name in any of Alexa's emails?" Leigh quickly asked.

"Not that she said. I don't think she's had time to go through them yet. This was just a quick report to say that she'd be looking for that particular connection." Yancy paused. "You think this guy had something to do with Alexa's murder?"

"That's what I intend to find out. I intend to question him after I've made a quick stop at my house for a change of clothes."

"Then you should probably take backup," Yancy said, the concern in his voice.

Leigh slid a glance to Cullen, maybe deciding that he could play backup if necessary. Maybe also calculating how long it would delay this visit if she had to wait for one of the other deputies to arrive.

"I have a license to carry," Cullen simply reminded her. "And you know I'm carrying." Though the reminder wasn't necessary since she'd seen him fire at the SUV that had attacked them.

"All right, I can legally deputize you," Leigh said after a short pause. "Temporarily deputize you," she emphasized.

Cullen didn't smile. Or curse. But he wasn't

sure how he felt about being a cop. Even a temporary one. Still, this was about protecting Leigh and getting answers, so he'd handle the deputy label for the next couple of hours.

Leigh started toward the door but then stopped and looked at Yancy. "If possible, arrange the interviews so that Kali and Austin aren't in here at the same time."

Yancy assured her that he would, and Cullen and she headed out, only to have Leigh stop again when she glanced around the parking lot. "My cruiser's wrecked," she muttered.

"We can take my truck," Cullen offered.

She didn't turn him down, though Cullen suspected she would have preferred to use an official vehicle for this visit with a suspect. Especially since she might have to arrest the man. But if that happened, Cullen's truck did have a narrow back seat they could use to transport him back to the police station.

Cullen deiced the windshield, noting that there were more people out and about now. People who noticed Leigh in the truck with him, and he wondered how much gossip and grief that was going to cause her.

"I'm muddying your reputation," Cullen joked, hoping to get a smile out of her.

No such luck. She looked at him with a slew of emotions crossing her face. Two of those emotions might have been frustration and regret, but there was also the heat.

"I would kiss you here and now just because I'm riled enough at the people who love picking my every move apart." Leigh took in a deep breath. "But that'd be using you."

Now he smiled. "If you kissed me, I'm positive that I'd feel plenty of things, but *used* isn't one of them."

She smiled, too, while shaking her head. Much to his disappointment though, she didn't kiss him.

Cullen drove to her place on the edge of town. Her one-story white limestone house sat in the center of four acres surrounded by white fence. A small red barn was behind the house, and he spotted a couple of bay mares inside. He'd known that Leigh was a horse lover, which wasn't a surprise since she'd been raised on a ranch.

He pulled up in front of her house, and both of them glanced around, looking for any signs of trouble, before she used her phone to disengage her security system. As they got out, Cullen pushed open the side of his jacket in case he had to go for his gun, but when Leigh unlocked the door and they went in, nothing seemed to be out of place.

"I won't be long," she said, leaving him in

the foyer. But she only made it a couple of steps before she turned back, caught onto him.

And she kissed him.

Cullen didn't even care that she'd chosen to do this behind closed doors. What he cared about was the instant slam of heat and need. The feel of her mouth. The pressure of her body against his. She didn't linger long, just enough to assure him that this attraction wasn't going away anytime soon.

Mumbling something he didn't catch, she pushed away from him and headed for the hall. "Help yourself to whatever you find in the fridge."

He wasn't the least bit interested in her fridge and considered going after her and seeing how far he could take things. Of course, he already knew that would just lead them to bed, and they couldn't take the time for that now. The sooner they got to Jimbo, the sooner they might have the answers they needed.

Forcing himself to go anywhere but to her bedroom, Cullen strolled into the living room. No fuss and frills here. There was a comfortable leather sofa the color of caramel, and from the looks of the way things were arranged, Leigh spent time in here reading, watching TV and working on a laptop that was open on a rustic coffee table.

He went to the fireplace to have a closer look at the single framed photograph on the mantel. A family shot of Cash, Leigh, their mother and their missing brother, Joe. It'd been taken when Leigh had been about five. That would have meant Cash was about seven and Joe three and a half. They were all smiling, and Cash was holding up a fish that he'd likely just caught.

It was a happy photo of a happy family, taken on a sunny summer day. There probably hadn't been many happy days after that because by Cullen's estimation, Joe had gone missing shortly afterward. A year later, Helen Mercer had died in a car accident that many had considered suicide. Losing her mother when she'd been so young was something they had in common.

"It used to hurt when I'd see that picture," Leigh said from behind him.

Cullen looked back at her, at the clean pair of jeans she was wearing. She'd also freed her hair from the ponytail, and it fell loose just below her shoulders.

"But now it gives me, well, comfort," she added. "Jeb took the picture. That's why he's not in it."

She probably didn't know that there was a tinge of bitterness in her tone when she said her father's name, and Cullen doubted that photo would be there for a daily reminder had Jeb actually been a visual part of the "happy" scene.

"You remember your mom?" he asked.

"Some. I have good memories, then the memories of her crying after Joe was taken." Leigh motioned for him to go with her to the door. "What about you? Do you remember your mother?"

"Some," he said, echoing her answer. And like Leigh, there were some good memories, but there'd been plenty of times when his mother had had way too much to drink. Something she'd done the night she died. As a child he couldn't see it. Now he knew she'd been an alcoholic. A mostly out-of-control one who'd made a habit of drinking and driving.

"You blame Bowen for her death?" Leigh asked.

"No." That was the truth. "But I love my father. Most of the time, anyway. So it's not something I talk about with him. Mostly though, I just blame my mother for not getting the help she obviously needed. Then again, I should put some of that blame on my dad, too, because he had to have known that the drinking had gotten way out of hand."

Leigh made a sound of agreement and added a genuine sounding "I'm sorry" as they went to his truck, and she reset the security system with her phone. She then gave him Jimbo's address so he could put it in the GPS.

"How much grief would your father give you…" But Leigh stopped and waved that off.

"How much grief would he give me if I started seeing you again?" Cullen finished for her. "Plenty," he readily admitted, "but that won't stop me. At this point, I doubt there's much of anything that'd stop us."

She didn't disagree with that, but the long breath she took let him know that she'd be getting plenty of grief as well.

"Your father approved of Alexa?" she asked.

Cullen nearly laughed when he recalled the many arguments Bowen and Alexa had had. "No. Not one little bit. He thought she had too much flash, too much temper."

Which was true, but Cullen had been attracted to her. That attraction was a drop in the bucket though compared to what he felt for Leigh. And he knew it was best to keep that to himself. He could coax Leigh into having an affair with him, but she wouldn't want to know how deep his feelings for her ran.

Cullen wasn't sure *he* wanted to know.

It had crushed him all the way to the bone, or rather the heart, the last time Leigh walked out of his life and he didn't want another round of that. Still, he was going to have to take the risk.

The roads were mostly clear and there was almost no traffic, but Cullen kept watch as they made their way out of Dark River and to the farm road that led to Jimbo's place. With each passing mile, Cullen's concerns grew, and he forced his mind off Leigh and back on the danger hanging over them.

"If Jimbo killed Alexa and was the one driving that SUV, he might try to finish us off," Cullen reminded her.

"Yes." She said it so fast that it'd obviously been on her mind. "I think the best way for us to do this is for me to call Jimbo when we get to his house. I'll insist that he come out so I can check him for weapons."

That was a good start, but Cullen wanted to go one step further. "You could question him while we're in the truck. That way, you're not out in the open in case he has a partner in crime."

She stayed quiet a moment. "Jimbo might not go for standing out in the cold while I talk to him."

"He might if he thinks this could lead to a payoff," Cullen quickly fired back.

Cullen gave her some time to work that around in her mind. Leigh finally nodded and took out her phone. She didn't press Jimbo's number though until Cullen took the final turn toward the farm.

And that's when Cullen saw the smoke.

There were dark coils of it rising into the sky, but the winter wind was whipping away at it, scattering it almost as soon as it rose. Since it was way too much smoke for an ordinary fireplace, Cullen got a very bad feeling in his gut.

"Jimbo's not answering," Leigh said, her attention focused on the smoke.

It was less than thirty seconds before they reached the house. Or rather what was left of it. The structure was engulfed in flames.

THE SIGHT OF those flames sent Leigh's stomach to her knees. In that instant, she knew the chances were very high that this wasn't an accidental fire.

And that Jimbo might be dead.

Because she doubted the man had set this fire. Then again, maybe he had if he'd thought he was about to be arrested for murder. There was a problem with that theory because of the truck parked in front of the house, and she was betting the truck belonged to Jimbo. Still, she wanted to hold out hope that he'd caught a ride with someone and torched his house to conceal any evidence inside.

Even though she didn't like the idea of a prime suspect being in the wind, it was better than the alternative of the man being dead. Dead men couldn't give her answers about those meetings with Alexa.

Since Leigh already had her phone in her hand, she called 911 to get the fire department out to Jimbo's house. But she could already see that they wouldn't get there in time to save the place.

She glanced around the yard, at the rusted-out farm equipment, overgrown trees and piles of junk. No Jimbo. In fact, no sign of anyone, but if he'd been attacked, then maybe he'd managed to make it outside before he would have been overcome by the smoke and fire.

"I'm keeping watch," Cullen assured her.

Leigh was already doing the same thing. Because even if Jimbo had been the one to set the fire, it was possible he'd stayed around to try to ambush them. That possibility, however, bit the dust when she saw Jimbo stagger out the front door.

The man's head and chest were bleeding, and he was clearly dazed. Added to that, his shirt was on fire.

Cullen and she threw open their doors at

the same time. They also drew their guns as one. Cullen sprinted across the yard toward Jimbo, catching onto him to take his weight and slapping out the fire with the sleeve of his coat. Leigh went to help, but she also looked all around the yard to make sure there was no other threat.

Jimbo mumbled something she couldn't understand and collapsed. If Cullen hadn't had hold of him, he would have fallen face-first to the ground. Cullen grabbed the man's arms, dragging him away from the house.

In the nick of time.

Because a chunk of the roof came crashing down and sent out a cloud of smoke, ash and cinders. When some of those cinders landed on Cullen, she had to use her own sleeve to stop them from igniting into full flames.

From the corner of her eye, she caught some movement to the right, but the wind shifted, sending the thick smoke right at them. She couldn't see her hand in front of her face much less someone who could be yards away. But the good news about that was the person might not be able to see them, either.

Leigh heard the sharp cracking sound, and for a split second she thought the rest of the house was collapsing. But then she knew what it was.

Gunfire.

Someone had just taken a shot at them, and the bullet tore into the ground just a few feet from where they were dragging Jimbo.

Cullen cursed, and he tried to shove Leigh behind him. "Get down," he snapped.

No way would Leigh do that. Not with someone shooting at them. She moved to take Jimbo's other arm to help Cullen drag him to the side of the truck so they'd have cover.

"Did you see the shooter?" Leigh asked Cullen. "I think he was running up from the right."

"I didn't see anyone," he said. His words rushed together with his heavy breath, and he peered over the front end of his truck. The shot came right away, skimming across the metal hood and slamming into a tree behind him. Cursing him, Leigh grabbed Cullen and forced him back down.

What he'd just done was way past being dangerous, but it'd helped pinpoint the direction of the shooter. He was in or near that area with the old farm equipment. Equipment that was plenty large enough to conceal whomever it was she'd glimpsed from the corner of her eye.

It had to be the killer.

But why hadn't he been in place to shoot them when they'd arrived? It would have been the perfect time since their attention was mostly focused on the burning house. Later, she'd give that some thought, but for now she needed to work on how to get them out of this.

They couldn't stay put. They were too close to the house, and it would collapse. No doubts about that. And when it went, some of those fiery chunks of wood could land on them. Plus, Jimbo was bleeding and needed medical attention ASAP. Leigh sent a quick text for an ambulance and backup.

More shots came, all of them slamming into the truck, but some of the bullets seemed to have come from different angles. The gunman could be on the move, maybe making his way to them so he could shoot them the moment he rounded the truck.

"Watch the front. I'll keep an eye on the rear," Leigh told Cullen.

Cullen dropped down on the ground next to Jimbo so he could look out underneath the truck. "He's coming this way," he snarled, and he shifted his gun to take aim.

Cullen fired.

The pain shot through Leigh's ears. It'd been necessary though. With the angle of his shot, Cullen would have likely only managed to wound the gunman in the leg, but that might be enough to stop him.

Cullen cursed again. "Smoke," he snapped.

That was the only warning Leigh got before another cloud of smoke came at them. It was thick and smothering, and it must have gotten to the gunman as well because she heard someone cough. And then she heard something else. More of the house collapsed, and the blazing debris landed between them and the shooter.

"I'm dying," Jimbo muttered, drawing her attention back to him. Unlike Cullen and her, he wasn't coughing, and the man seemed to be on his last breath.

Leigh needed him alive, and the only chance they had was to get him to a hospital fast. She reached up, fumbling for the door, and opened it as wide as she could manage.

"Get in and stay down," Cullen told her through his coughs.

"You do the same," she insisted.

She took hold of Jimbo's arm, and while Cullen and she both tried to keep watch, they hauled the man into the center of the seat. Cullen quickly followed, getting behind the wheel. He threw the truck into Reverse and gunned the engine.

Leigh braced herself for the hail of gunfire.

But it didn't come.

Still, she kept her gun ready while Cullen sped out of the driveway. Once they were out of the cloud of smoke, she looked around, trying to pick through the yard to spot the person who'd just tried to kill them.

Nothing.

The shooter was nowhere in sight.

Chapter Eleven

Cullen could feel the exhaustion all the way to his bones, and he figured it was the same for Leigh. They were both dragging when they walked into her house, nearly ten hours after they'd left to do the interview with Jimbo. What was supposed to have been a short trip had turned into a grueling ordeal. One that could have ended with Leigh and him dead.

Like Jimbo.

Despite their efforts to save him, Jimbo had died shortly after they'd arrived at the hospital. He hadn't been able to tell anyone who'd put the two bullets in his chest that'd killed him. And with his house a total loss, his killer hadn't left any evidence behind. In fact, he'd left nothing behind. The local cops hadn't been able to find him or a vehicle he'd used to get to Jimbo's. It was as if the guy had vanished like the smoke from the fire.

At least during the ten hours, Leigh's deputies had done the interviews with Austin and Kali. According to the updates Leigh had gotten, neither had given any new info, but the interviews ticked off some necessary legal boxes. So had the searches of both Kali's and her parents' houses. Some blue dresses had been collected at both and had been sent to the lab.

"The bathroom's there," Leigh said, motioning toward the hall. "The guest room's right next to it." She glanced at his jeans and shirt that were stained with Jimbo's blood. "I'll see if I can find you something to wear while you wash those. The laundry room's just off the kitchen."

Cullen wasn't sure if he wanted to think about why she'd have men's clothes in her house, and he sure as heck wasn't going to press on getting something from the Triple R. According to Mack, the ranch was still being processed as a crime scene, and the CSIs didn't want anything removed until they were finished.

Leigh glanced down at her own clothes, at the blood there, and she groaned softly. It didn't matter that Jimbo had been a thug with a long criminal history. A man was dead, and he'd almost certainly died because Alexa's killer had wanted to tie up any loose ends.

But how had the killer known to go after Jimbo?

That was a question that'd been circling in Cullen's mind. No doubt circling in Leigh's, too.

"Help yourself to anything in the kitchen," she added. "Once you're done with your shower, let me know, and I'll take one."

Neither of them moved, and exhaustion was only part of the reason why. Cullen could practically feel the guilt coming off her.

"You couldn't have saved Jimbo," Cullen insisted.

"I could have if I'd realized the killer would go after him." She muttered some profanity and then groaned. "I should have realized it. I should have asked the locals to provide him protection until I could get out to his place."

He could have reminded her that she'd been embroiled in a murder investigation and that she was functioning on very little sleep. But she'd see that as part of the job so he saved his breath. Instead, he went to her and pulled her into his arms. Maybe it was the exhaustion playing into this again, but she didn't resist. She went body to body with him and dropped her head on his shoulder.

Cullen knew she was allowing this because she needed some comfort, and there weren't exactly a lot of people in Dark River who could offer her that. Heck, he needed what she was giving as well. It'd been a damn long day, and it felt good to stand there with her like this.

"Don't kiss me," she said. "I don't have the willpower to do anything about it."

Cullen managed to laugh. "That's probably not something you should tell me."

"Yes, it is," Leigh argued. "Because underneath all that bad boy, you're a decent guy."

Well, hell. How could he kiss her after she'd said that? And yes, he had indeed been thinking about a kiss or two. Nothing more though. When they ended up having sex again, he wanted them to have enough energy to enjoy it. Still, Cullen settled for brushing a kiss on her forehead because there was indeed some bad boy beneath the decency.

The kiss caused her to chuckle a little, and she stepped back to meet his gaze. Mercy, she was beautiful even now with those tired eyes.

"You're not thinking about sex, are you?" he asked, hoping that she'd managed to get a second wind.

"No." The corner of her mouth lifted in a smile. A smile that quickly faded. "I was thinking about how the killer knew to go after Jimbo."

So, her mind had indeed been toying with that.

"Let me change my clothes," she added a

moment later, "and then I'd like to hear your theories on how that could have happened." She went into her bedroom but didn't close the door all the way. "I'm thinking Alexa could have told her killer about Jimbo. Maybe she did that in passing, and then the killer might have decided that Alexa could have told Jimbo about him or her."

Cullen could see that happening with Austin or Kali. Austin because he was having an affair with Alexa, and Kali because Alexa was her friend. He'd heard Leigh talking on the phone with Yancy, and the deputy had taken both Austin's and Kali's statements, and it'd be interesting to see if there was any connection to Jimbo.

When the killer was finally identified and locked up, Cullen knew he was also going to have to deal with the impact of his best friend having a relationship with his ex. Even though Cullen had no longer loved Alexa, the affair still felt like a betrayal. One that he'd need to process. Process and then hopefully put aside since he had a lot of things to deal with. That included his feelings for Leigh.

"Or maybe Jimbo had a partner," Leigh added a moment later, "and the partner killed him rather than risk Jimbo tying him or her to a murder."

Despite the seriousness of the conversation, it took Cullen a moment to focus on something other than remembering Leigh and her beautiful, tired eyes from moments ago. "Either of those are possible," he said, leaning against the wall outside her door. "But Rocky would have gotten the preliminary report that your other deputy sent out. He knew you'd be earmarking any emails or texts between Alexa and Jimbo."

He had no trouble hearing her quick sound of agreement which meant that had already occurred to her.

"This rules out your father," Leigh went on. "He knew about Jimbo before Alexa's murder, and if he was a killer, he probably wouldn't have waited hours to eliminate someone who could have incriminated him."

"Bowen will be pleased to hear that." And yeah, he added a little tongue and cheek to that comment.

"Jeb won't be pleased." Leigh had a tongue-in-cheek tone, too.

At the mention of her father's name, Cullen recalled what'd happened in the break room when Jeb had had the dizzy spell. Or whatever the heck it'd been. He nearly brought it up now, but Leigh continued before he could say anything.

"But I'd prefer to arrest the person responsible rather than the person I want it to be," she said, and he heard her sigh.

"You want it to be Rocky," he concluded. "He's withheld evidence and backbites you any chance he gets."

"And that's why I'm being very careful about how I'm dealing with him. I don't want to project something on him that might not be there. He might not be more than just a back-biter."

She opened the door, and he saw that she was wearing a white terry cloth bathrobe. It wasn't clinging, low-cut or anything else provocative, but it still got his attention.

Before he could give in to the temptation of sliding his hand inside that robe, she thrust out a pair of black pj bottoms.

"Sorry," she said. "It's the best I can do. Cash stayed here about six years ago when his house was being painted, and he left them behind. Just the bottoms," Leigh clarified. "So, you'll have to do the bare-chest thing while your clothes are being washed."

He was about to joke and ask her if she'd be watching for that, but her doorbell rang. Leigh whirled around, scooping up her holster. At the same time, Cullen also drew his gun.

"I doubt the killer would ring the doorbell," he said, trying to steady her nerves. But Cullen didn't plan on putting his gun away until he was sure who was at the door.

Cullen went to one of the side windows. Leigh went to the other. And they both groaned when they spotted Austin on her porch.

"I have to talk to you," Austin called out, ringing the bell again.

"I'll get rid of him," Cullen offered, and he didn't wait for Leigh to object.

He held on to his gun as he opened the door and faced his friend. That would be *former* friend since one look at Austin and Cullen knew Austin was still riled. Heck, Cullen was, too.

"Where's Leigh?" Austin demanded.

With just those two words, Cullen got a whiff of Austin's breath. He'd clearly been drinking.

"What do you want?" Leigh asked, moving in front of Cullen to face Austin head-on.

"Kali thinks I murdered Alexa," Austin blurted out, pointing his index finger at Leigh. "You made her believe that."

Hell. This was not what Leigh needed to be dealing with after the day they'd already had. "Leigh was doing her job," Cullen quickly pointed out. "And you didn't exactly volunteer information about your affair with Alexa."

Austin's rage-filled eyes slashed to Cullen.

"Because it was my personal business. My mistake. There was no reason for me to tell a cop."

"No," Leigh disagreed. "There's no such thing as personal business in a murder investigation."

"Have you tried to ruin Cullen the way you're ruining me?" Austin fired back. Then, he smirked. "No, you haven't because you're sleeping with him again." He gave a hollow laugh. "Alexa was right about that."

Cullen stared at Austin. "What do you mean by that?"

Austin continued the smirk. "Alexa saw you looking at an old picture of the two of you. The one taken at a party when Leigh was still in high school."

The party where Leigh had lost her virginity to him. Cullen did indeed have a picture, but he didn't remember looking at it while Alexa was around.

"Alexa was so jealous of you," Austin continued, his comment aimed at Leigh. "And she had a vindictive streak and wouldn't have wanted Cullen and you to be together. I could have sent her after you like that." He snapped his fingers. "Too bad I didn't. If I had, you wouldn't have ruined my life."

Enough was enough. Cullen stepped in front

of Leigh again. "You ruined your own life," Cullen snarled. "By not keeping your jeans zipped when you were around your fiancée's best friend. If you want to put the blame on someone, just look in the mirror."

Austin clearly didn't care much for that, and he reached out as if he might try to clamp onto Leigh's arm. Cullen didn't let that happen. The punch he landed on Austin's jaw was hard and fast. Austin staggered back, the blood already oozing from his mouth, and he glared at Cullen.

"You two deserve each other," Austin snarled, and weaving, he started off the porch and toward his truck in the driveway.

Leigh sighed, took out her phone. "You've been drinking," she called out to Austin, "and you're not getting behind the wheel. We have a couple of people in town doing Uber, and I'll get you a ride."

"I don't want a ride," he insisted, although he didn't get in his truck. He started walking back toward town. Cullen was about to go after him, but he saw the truck approaching the house.

"Great," Leigh muttered. "It's Jeb."

Cullen hadn't thought this day could get any worse, but he'd apparently been wrong. Jeb stopped his truck next to Austin and lowered the window. Cullen couldn't hear what they said, but they had a very short conversation before Austin got in the passenger's seat.

Jeb drove to the house, got out and was sporting a serious scowl as he walked to the porch. "I'll see that Austin gets to the inn. There should be rooms open by now."

"Thanks," Cullen said, and he was glad Jeb was seeing to this. Austin was in no shape to drive or walk in the cold.

Jeb didn't acknowledge Cullen's thanks. In fact, he didn't acknowledge Cullen at all. He stared at his daughter.

"I came to give you a heads-up," Jeb said. "Rocky's asked the town council to have a meeting tomorrow. You'll need to be there."

"And why would I need to do that?" Leigh asked.

Jeb swore under his breath and scrubbed his hand over his face. "Because Rocky's going to present what he says is evidence to have you removed as sheriff."

LEIGH READ THROUGH the CSI and ME reports and tried to stay focused. Hard to do because she'd had yet another night with little sleep.

Cullen probably hadn't fared much better in the sleep department, and he looked as tired as she was as he worked on a laptop in her living room. She wanted to tell him to take a break, especially since she'd have to be heading into her office soon, but he was going through the photos that the deputies had collected from the party guests. Those photos might end up holding some clues as to what had happened that night.

She desperately needed answers. Desperately needed the attacks to stop before anyone else died. She could still feel Jimbo's blood on her hands. Could still hear the sound of gunfire.

She pushed back what would have been a shudder, drank her coffee and kept reading. Basically, there was no news in either report that she could use to make an arrest, but the ME had concluded that Alexa had recently had sex. That didn't necessarily mean that sex had been with Austin, but Leigh would need to take another look at Cullen's friend. Before she did that though, she wanted the lab results on the clothes that'd been taken from Austin's house. There was no telling when those would be processed, but she'd give the lab a call and try to hurry them.

If she had a job, that is.

She tried not to think that she could lose her badge today. It could happen though. She doubted that Rocky had any actual evidence to present to the town council, but he could use her connection with Cullen. That was a darn good reason for her to put some distance between Cullen and her. But if she did that, it would be for all the wrong reasons—because she'd been pressured into it.

There were right reasons for distancing herself. A possible broken heart and butting heads with Bowen. However, one look at Cullen, and Leigh knew she didn't exactly have a choice about her feelings for him.

"Problem?" Cullen asked, and that was when Leigh realized he'd caught her staring at him.

She waved that off just as her phone rang. "Jeb," she muttered and hit the decline button. Leigh wasn't in the mood for a lecture or advice.

Cullen stood, facing her, and he crammed his hands in the pockets of his jeans. It seemed to her that he was having a debate about what he wanted to say. "Is your father okay?" he asked.

Of all the things Leigh had thought Cullen might say, that wasn't one of them. And his tone only added to her surprise. He seemed concerned, and that didn't mesh with his usual feelings about Jeb.

"Why do you ask?" she countered, and she hoped this wasn't about to turn into a discussion of whether or not Jeb could have killed Alexa and Jimbo.

Again, Cullen hesitated. He shook his head, then huffed. "Jeb wanted me to swear not to tell you, but he had a dizzy spell yesterday in the break room. It happened shortly after you left for your office."

Everything inside Leigh went still while she tried to wrap her mind around that. "A dizzy spell?"

Cullen nodded. "He went pale and staggered back before I caught him. If he hadn't told me to keep it from you, I might have dismissed it as nothing. But it feels like something," he added.

Yes, it did, and Leigh tried to wrap her mind around that, too. Was Jeb sick? Or was it worse than that? Either way, she could see him wanting to keep it from her. Maybe because he didn't want her thinking he was weak. Or perhaps because it was just something he wanted to keep to himself. Neither of those excuses would work on her. Jeb and she might not be close, but she wanted to know if he was having health problems.

Leigh pressed Jeb's number, and since he'd just tried to call her, she expected him to answer. He didn't. In fact, it went to voice mail, but before she could leave him a message, she got an incoming call from the reserve deputy Cecile Taggart.

"Is everything okay with Jamie?" Leigh immediately asked.

"He's fine. In fact, the doctor might let him go home late today or tomorrow."

Leigh released the breath she was holding. That was good news. No one had tried to kill Jamie again, but his release would pose a few new problems. She'd need to get with Cullen on that and see how they could protect him while he was on the Triple R.

"I was calling about those emails and phone records you wanted me to check," Cecile continued a moment later. "Alexa's emails and phone records," she explained. "I've been going through them, and I think I found something."

"I'm listening," Leigh assured her, and she was. So was Cullen, who'd moved closer to her. Leigh put the call on speaker so he'd be able to hear.

"Well, it might be nothing, but there's a text from Alexa to Kali Starling where Alexa confesses that she's having an affair with Kali's fiancé."

Leigh was reasonably sure this wasn't *nothing*. "When did Alexa send that?"

"About four hours before the start of the

party," Cecile quickly answered. "It appears Alexa deleted some other texts from her sent folder but not this one."

"Did Kali respond to the text?"

"Not with a text, but there's a record of an incoming call from Kali shortly after she would have gotten the text."

Leigh groaned. It would have been better to have that particular conversation in writing, but maybe Kali could fill in the blanks. "I want you to forward me that text," Leigh instructed.

"Will do, but there's more. Vance and Dawn have been going through the pictures of the guests at the party. I don't think it's my imagination that Kali looks pretty upset in several of them. In one, she looks sort of disheveled. Windblown, I guess you'd say. Her hair is a little messy, and she looks as if she's been crying."

Interesting, and Leigh very much wanted to know what Kali had to say about that. She ended the call with Cecile and immediately contacted Kali. Leigh almost expected the woman to dodge her, but she answered.

"Kali, one of my deputies just went through Alexa's texts," Leigh said, going right to the heart of the matter. "Anything you want to tell me that you left out of your interview?"

"W-what?" Kali answered, slurring the word.

"Alexa's texts," Leigh repeated.

Kali moaned softly. "Uh, I can't think right now." That was slurred, too.

"Kali, are you all right?" Leigh demanded.

There were more moans. "Sleeping now. I took something to help me sleep." And with that, the woman ended the call.

Leigh cursed and immediately contacted dispatch. "I need someone to go to Kali Starling's residence and do a welfare check. Make it fast," she told the dispatcher. "It's possible the woman has overdosed on sleeping pills."

If she had, hopefully help wouldn't be late in getting there.

"Would Kali try to kill herself?" Leigh asked Cullen.

He lifted his shoulder. "I don't know. But if you think it'll be a while before someone can get to her place, I'll go."

Leigh considered it, then shook her head. "If Kali's the killer, this could be a trap." And that was something Leigh relayed to the dispatcher when she called him back.

She'd just put her phone away when there was a knock at her door. Heck, what now? Frustrated, she went to the side window, looked out and spotted Jeb. He must have known she would peer out like that because his gaze zoomed right to hers.

"I need to see you," he said.

Leigh looked at him, studying his face to see if there were any signs of the paleness and staggering that Cullen had described. Nothing out of the ordinary except his eyes were tired. Then again, her eyes were probably tired, too.

She went to the door and opened it. "I'm not up to a long visit," she said, "but I do have questions for you."

With his mouth tightening, Jeb shifted his attention to Cullen. "If something's wrong with you, Leigh should know," Cullen told him.

"No time for that," Jeb insisted, turning back to Leigh. "The mayor just called, and he's assembled the town council. You're about to get a call from him, and he'll tell you that they want you there right now."

Chapter Twelve

Cullen thought the mood in the town hall felt like a witch hunt. And he was pretty sure that at least some of the council considered Leigh to be the witch. But Cullen hoped that Rocky hadn't been able to turn all of them against the woman the majority of residents had elected sheriff.

"If the town council votes to start the process to oust you," Jeb explained as they paused outside the door of the meeting room, "it wouldn't be immediate."

Leigh nodded. "They'd have to initiate a recall." Her jaw was tight. Eyes, narrowed. "The voters would have to decide if I should stay or go."

Cullen couldn't blame her for being riled to the core. He knew how much the badge meant to her, and how devastated she'd be if it was taken away.

Leigh stepped ahead of them and opened the

door. She didn't hesitate but instead walked into the room and went straight to the front. The mayor, Noble Henning, was there at the center of the rectangular table, and part of his mayoral duties was to head the council. He was flanked by the five other members who made up the town council. Those other members were business owners or prominent citizens—which explained why Jeb was on it. He took his seat at the far end of the table.

Noble was a huge man with an equally huge belly. Since he was a rancher, Cullen had done business with him and had found him fair enough. Right now though, nothing felt fair, and Cullen cursed Noble, Rocky and everyone at the council table for putting Leigh through this.

Rocky was there in the front row, and he made a point of staring at Leigh as she stood in front of the people who could decide her fate. Word of the meeting apparently hadn't gotten out because other than the mayor and the members of the council, Rocky was the only other person there.

Cullen stayed at the back of the room, but Leigh went all the way to the table to face the council along with giving Rocky a cold, hard glance that was effective enough to cause him to look away.

Noble cleared his throat and also had some trouble looking Leigh in the eye. Instead, he read from his notes. "Sheriff Mercer, there have been complaints and concerns about you being negligent in carrying out your duties in the murders you're currently investigating. Deputy Rocky Callaway claims you've shown preferential treatment to a suspect and have failed to arrest that suspect because you're having a sexual relationship with him."

That got Cullen moving forward, but Leigh spoke before he could say anything.

"I'm assuming that my deputy is referring to Cullen Brodie." Leigh's voice was calm, but Cullen suspected there was no calmness beneath the surface.

Noble nodded just as Rocky blurted out, "You should have arrested Cullen instead of sleeping with him."

"There was no evidence to make that arrest," Leigh countered, turning her attention back to the mayor. "Cullen's clothes were taken to the lab and there was no blood on them. The CSIs used a UV light on other clothes in his closet and didn't detect any blood. According to the assessment of the crime scene, the killer would have gotten some blood spatter on themselves."

"Cullen was alone with the body—" Rocky started, but the mayor motioned for him to hush.

"The lab is still testing the clothing of others who attended the party," Leigh continued without missing a beat, "and once I have those results I might be able to make an arrest if the evidence warrants that. There are several people who have means, motive and opportunity, and some, including Deputy Callaway, weren't forthcoming with information about the victim."

Rocky practically jumped to his feet. "I wasn't forthcoming because it wasn't relevant."

"I decide what's relevant in a murder investigation." Leigh tapped her badge. "And you failed to tell me about a meeting you had with the victim."

Noble made another motion for Rocky to sit back down. The deputy did after several snail-crawling moments. Then, Noble's gaze shifted to Cullen.

"I'm guessing you've got something you want to say to the council?" Noble asked.

Cullen was certain his body language conveyed that, yes, he did have something to say. He wanted to tell them all to go to hell and take the backstabbing Rocky with them. But that venom wouldn't help Leigh.

"I'm not especially happy that any one of you would think I'd need to sleep with the sheriff in order to keep myself out of jail,"

Cullen snarled. "It especially pisses me off that you'd think Leigh would sleep with someone she believes could bash in a woman's head."

"Are you saying you haven't shared the sheriff's bed?" Noble asked.

"I'm saying it's none of your business," he snapped at the same time Leigh said, "Cullen's not a suspect so you don't have cause to ask that question."

Rocky smirked, obviously pleased because he probably thought Leigh was digging herself into a huge hole.

The door practically flew open, and Vance, Dawn and Yancy all came rushing in. They glanced around the room as if assessing the situation and then went to the front to stand by Leigh.

"Sorry," Vance said, "but we just got the word that the sheriff was having some trouble here. We didn't want her facing that trouble alone."

Leigh made eye contact with all three of them and nodded her appreciation. "Thank you," she said plenty loud enough for everyone in the room to hear.

"The *trouble* is," Noble spoke up, emphasizing the word, "the sheriff doesn't seem to be close to arresting anybody for murder."

"She's had less than two days," Cullen argued and got sounds and mumbles of agreement from the three deputies standing with her. "You want her to arrest the wrong person just so you'll have someone behind bars? I don't think you want that kind of justice doled out here."

"No, I don't want the wrong person arrested," Noble countered, "but I want the threat gone. I want people to know they're safe in their own homes."

"This might help," Vance said, and he handed Leigh a piece of paper.

She read through what was written on it, and while she didn't smile, Cullen thought he saw some relief. "The SUV that rammed into my cruiser was sent to the lab for processing," Leigh relayed to the council. "The steering wheel had been wiped, but they found a partial print. The lab's going to try to match it."

Noble blew out what Cullen thought might be a breath of relief. "Good," he said. "Then, we'll postpone this meeting until you've had a chance to get the match."

It didn't seem nearly enough. More postponing the witch hunt rather than giving Leigh the credit she was due.

Jeb stood as if he might say something for, or against, his daughter, but Leigh's attention wasn't on her father. Or anyone else on the council. It was on her phone as it rang.

"It's Austin," she relayed in a whisper to Cullen and her three standing deputies. While Noble officially ended the meeting, Leigh stepped to the side of the room to take the call. Cullen went with her.

"Something's happened to Kali," he heard Austin blurt out.

Cullen thought of the part of the phone conversation he'd heard when Leigh had been talking to Kali. Leigh had been concerned enough to send someone out to check on the woman.

"What's wrong?" Leigh demanded.

"I came to her house to check on her, but she's not here." Austin groaned. "And there's blood on her back porch. Leigh, you need to come right away."

LEIGH HAD PLENTY on her mind as Cullen and she hurried out of the town hall toward his truck. She still had plenty of anger about the town council meeting that Rocky had been able to wrangle. Plenty of anger directed at Rocky, too. But right now, her focus was on Kali.

She certainly hadn't forgotten about her brief conversation with Kali, and Leigh had suspected then that the woman was in some kind of trouble. Not the kind of trouble that would cause blood to be on her porch though. No. However, Leigh knew this could have turned out to be an overdose, either accidental or intentional.

"Where are you now?" Leigh asked Austin.

"I'm trying to figure out a way inside Kali's house. She must have changed the locks because my key doesn't work, and all the windows are locked up."

It didn't surprise her that Kali would change the locks. The woman had been very upset over Austin's cheating. But that led Leigh to another question. "Why call me and not the locals?"

"Uh, I don't know the locals," Austin answered. "I know you."

Yes, and it was a huge understatement to say he didn't much care for her. Still, it was possible this wasn't a trap and had nothing to do with his feelings about her. Maybe Austin was truly panicked about Kali, and he would have had her phone number right there in his contacts.

"Call an ambulance," Leigh instructed Austin, "but don't go in." Because if this wasn't an overdose, it could be another murder. The killer could still be inside. "There should be someone from Clay Ridge PD arriving soon. Tell him or her what you just told me."

She ended the call and instructed her own deputies—Vance, Yancy and Dawn—to go back to whatever needed to be done, that she would handle things with Kali. Then, Leigh called her brother, and she was thankful when Cash answered right away.

"One of my deputies, Karen Wheatly, should be at Kali's house soon," Cash said without any kind of greeting. "I'm guessing that's why you're calling?"

"I am," Leigh confirmed. The moment they'd buckled up, Cullen took off, heading out of town. "Her former fiancé is there now, and he says there's blood on the porch."

Cash cursed. "The dispatcher didn't say there were any signs of foul play or danger so I didn't send any backup with Karen."

"I just now found out about the blood, and Cullen and I are on the way there now," Leigh assured him. "Call your deputy and tell her to approach with caution. The same person who killed Jimbo could have gone after Kali."

Cash belted out some more profanity. "I'm in Lubbock right now and won't be able to get there for at least thirty minutes. You'll be backing up my deputy?"

"I will. I'll keep you posted," she added

and ended the call. Leigh immediately started glancing around, no doubt to make sure they weren't about to be attacked.

"Are you okay?" Cullen asked, but he, too, kept watch.

It took Leigh a couple of seconds to shift gears from her conversation with Cash, but she knew what Cullen was really asking. He wanted to know how she was handling what had just happened in the town hall.

"If I don't make an arrest soon, the mayor could press for a recall and have me ousted from office," she said. "Rocky might have been the one to set everything in motion, but Noble will get pressure, and he just might cave."

Still, Noble wouldn't be able to start the recall process to get rid of her by himself. It would take a majority vote from the council. Leigh had no idea just how many, or how few, votes would swing her way. Heck, she couldn't even count on getting Jeb's support. But that wouldn't stop her from doing her job for as long as she held the badge.

"I know you won't want it, but Bowen could put some pressure on Noble," Cullen offered.

She gave him a thin smile. "You're right. I don't want it." She paused. "But thanks. Right now, you and the three deputies who showed up are my biggest supporters."

The sound of agreement that Cullen made let her know that he was more than that. Yes, he was. Even though they weren't lovers, Leigh knew that would soon change. She'd land in bed with him, but she needed to keep her heart and the heat in check until after she'd finished this murder investigation.

Thankfully, the temps had warmed up enough that most of the ice was gone so the trip to Clay Ridge didn't take that long. Good thing, too, because Kali didn't live in town as Leigh had expected. According to the background data Leigh pulled up on her phone, Kali's house was situated on ten acres where she had horses. And it wasn't a sprawling, expensive place, either. The white frame house looked simple and cozy.

When Cullen pulled into the driveway, she spotted the cruiser and the lanky female deputy who was in the front yard with Austin. Leigh immediately looked to see if he was armed. He didn't have a gun in his hand, but that didn't mean he wasn't carrying one beneath his bulky coat.

"The blood's back here," Austin said the moment Leigh and Cullen were out of his truck. He motioned for them to follow him. But Leigh took a moment to introduce herself and Cullen to Deputy Karen Wheatly.

"I haven't been here long," Karen explained, "but Mr. Borden's right about the blood. There are some drops on the back porch."

"Drops," Leigh repeated. That was better than a huge amount, but it was still troublesome. "You haven't been inside?"

"I was about to do that now. I've knocked on the door, and Kali hasn't responded so that and the blood gives me probable cause to break the lock."

It did indeed, but before Leigh could ask if the deputy had a crowbar with her, Cullen pulled out a utility knife from his pocket. "I can get us in."

He didn't wait for permission, either. With Austin right on his heels and telling him to hurry, Cullen went to the front door. He had the lock open within a matter of seconds.

"Nick," Cullen said as an explanation.

Since his brother, Nick, was an ATF agent, Leigh figured that he'd taught Cullen how to get through locks. She was glad Noble or Rocky hadn't been around to see him use those skills or they probably would have considered it more reason for her to arrest him.

They stepped into the house, and Leigh noted that no security alarm went off. Maybe Kali had disengaged it. It wasn't a large place, but all the furniture appeared to be high-end.

There also didn't seem to be anything out of place. Definitely no signs of a struggle.

"Kali?" Austin called out, and he would have bolted toward the hall had Cullen not took hold of him.

"It might not be safe," Cullen warned him.

"But Kali could be hurt," Austin insisted.

He slung off Cullen's grip. However, he waited, going with Karen, Leigh and Cullen as they went through the place room by room. Like the other parts of the house, there was nothing to indicate there'd been a problem.

Until they reached the kitchen.

There were what appeared to be drops of blood on the floor. Again, it wasn't a large amount and there was no spatter on the walls or counters to indicate blunt force trauma.

"The back door's locked," Karen pointed out.

Yes, and that was puzzling. The blood clearly led toward the door so if Kali had been attacked or hurt, why would she or her attacker take the time to lock up behind them?

Karen unlocked the door, and stepping around the blood, they went onto the back porch. More drops here, and these would have been the ones that Austin and Karen had already spotted. Leigh hoped that Austin hadn't compromised the scene by touching anything.

As it was, he was going to be a suspect if anything had happened to Kali, and it'd be worse for him if he'd left traces of himself behind.

Leigh went down the steps, spotting a few more blood drops on the brown winter grass. She continued a few more feet, but when Leigh didn't see any more blood, she stopped and glanced around.

Kali's place was a lot like Leigh's. There was a small barn, what appeared to be a storage shed and plenty of fenced pastures. There was a heavily treed area to the right and a creek on the left. Leigh felt her stomach tighten because she didn't want Kali to have ended up in the icy water. Austin must have had that same thought because he started to run in that direction.

"I'll go with him," Karen insisted. "Why don't you two have a look around the barn?"

Leigh nodded, but before she moved, she spoke to Karen in a whisper. "I'm not sure I can trust Austin so watch your back."

Karen's eyes widened a little when she glanced at Austin. "Thanks." She slid her hand over the butt of her weapon and went after him.

Leigh continued to keep an eye on Austin until Cullen and she made it to the barn. Both drew their guns and stepped inside. She went still, listening, but didn't hear anything. She also didn't see any signs of blood.

"This doesn't make sense," Leigh muttered. She was hoping if she spoke her thoughts aloud that Cullen could help her understand what'd gone on here. "If Kali was taken, why would her kidnapper have brought her out through the back door? Why wouldn't he have just put her in his vehicle?"

They stepped out of the barn, and Cullen tipped his head to the woods. "There are probably trails out there where the kidnapper could have left his vehicle." He stopped and shook his head. "But it's a long way to take an injured woman. Especially since none of her neighbors are close enough to see if he'd taken her out through the front."

True, and that left Leigh with an unsettling theory. "If Kali tried to kill herself, she could have maybe staggered out of the house and collapsed somewhere." In this bitter cold, she wouldn't last long.

"The shed." Cullen motioned toward it, and that's when Leigh noticed the door was slightly ajar.

Mercy. Was Kali in there? Hurt and maybe hiding?

"Kali?" Leigh called out. "It's Sheriff Mercer. Cullen's with me. Do you need help?"

When Leigh got no answer, Cullen and she started in that direction. But they didn't get far.

Only a couple of steps. Before they heard the scream. Not coming from the shed but rather from the woods.

"Kali," Leigh said on a rise of breath, and they began running toward the scream.

The shot rang out before they even made it past the shed.

Leigh was already moving to take cover, but Cullen hurried that along. He took hold of her, dragging her back behind the shed. Just as another shot blasted through the air.

Her adrenaline kicked in. So did the memories of the shooting just the day before. A shooting where Cullen and she had come close to dying. Hard to not let that play into this now, but Leigh battled the fear and forced herself to focus.

"The shot came from the woods," she said.

"Yeah, and it sounded like a rifle," Cullen agreed. "I'm pretty sure it came from the same area as the scream."

Leigh believed that, too, and it could mean that Kali had just been shot. Or worse. Killed. Her instincts were to go after Kali, to try to save her. But that would be suicide, and it could get Cullen killed, too, because there was no way he'd let her go out there alone.

"Kali?" Leigh called out again.

Her voice would give away their position, but the shooter probably already knew their exact location. She got confirmation of that when more shots came, and all of them smacked into the storage shed.

Cullen cursed and dragged Leigh to the ground, until they were practically on their bellies. Leigh only hoped that Karen and Austin were also taking cover.

"Kali?" Leigh tried again, not expecting the woman to answer.

And that's why it surprised Leigh when she did.

"I'm here!" Kali shouted. She was definitely in the woods. "Someone's trying to kill me."

Welcome to the club. Since the shots all seemed to be coming right at the shed, maybe that meant the gunman wasn't actually firing at Kali. Then again, if the shooter had injured her and taken her into the woods, it was possible Kali was the target and the guy was just missing.

But Leigh didn't believe that.

No. The bullets were coming too close for them not to be in the crosshairs of this snake.

"Help me!" Kali shouted.

"Get down!" Leigh yelled back. "Take cover."

"I'll create a diversion," Cullen said. "I'll get the shooter to focus on me."

Leigh didn't even get the chance to say no to that because Cullen got up and hurried to the back end of the shed. He kept low, but Leigh knew it wouldn't be nearly low enough for the bullets that were still coming their way.

"Don't do this," Leigh snapped.

He didn't listen. Cullen peeled off his jacket, and he thrust it out from cover. It drew immediate gunfire and sent Leigh's heart into a tailspin. Mercy. He was making himself a target, and if the shots went just a little to the left, they'd hit Cullen.

Hurrying, she crawled to him, took hold of his leg and jerked him back down. Cullen didn't go easily. He was obviously still hellbent on saving Kali because he tossed out his jacket, probably with the idea of drawing gunfire while Kali managed to take cover.

But the shots stopped.

Suddenly, it was quiet, and the only sounds were their ragged breaths and her pulse throbbing in her ears.

"He's getting away again," Leigh murmured.

She groaned and punched the shed with the side of her fist. The frustration and anger washed over her. Catching the shooter was the only way to stop these attacks. The only way to stop him from killing again. But part of her was relieved, too. If the shots stopped, then Cullen wouldn't be gunned down.

"Don't ever do anything like that again," she snapped. At least she'd intended to snap, but her voice was too breathy and her words too broken.

Cullen looked at her. But he didn't nod or make any sounds of agreement. Instead, he kissed her. It was hard, fast and like another punch of adrenaline.

"Sheriff Mercer?" Karen called out. "Are you both okay?"

"Yes." Leigh had to steady herself to add more. "What about Austin and you?"

"I'm fine. Not sure about Austin. He got away from me before I could even get to the creek. I don't know where he went."

Cullen's gaze met hers, and in his eyes, Leigh could see the same emotions that were no doubt in hers. Damn. This wasn't good. Leigh hated to think the worst about the man, but it was possible Austin had planted a rifle before Cullen, the deputy or she arrived, and he could have been the one to fire the shots.

"Any signs of the shooter?" Leigh asked the deputy.

"No. And none of the shots came my way."

"Good. Stay put until we're sure it's clear."

But the words had barely left her mouth when Leigh heard Austin. "I found her," he shouted. "I found Kali."

Chapter Thirteen

Cullen steeled himself, preparing for the worst when he saw Kali. But she was nowhere in the "worst" category.

He saw that right away when Kali came running out of the woods.

Leigh, Karen and he all started toward her. Kali's hair was disheveled, and there were smudges of dirt on her face, but he couldn't see any injuries that would have left those blood drops.

"Kali, wait!" Austin called out to her.

But Kali kept running, and she practically collapsed into Cullen's arms when he caught her. "I don't want Austin here."

In the grand scheme of things, that seemed small compared to everything else that had just happened. And to everything that could still happen. The shooter could still be out there, ready to fire off more shots, and that's why

Cullen led Kali to the side of the shed so they'd have some cover.

"Are you hurt?" Leigh asked her.

With her breath gusting, Kali nodded. Then shook her head. She lifted her hand, to show them the gash on her palm. "I cut myself in the kitchen." It was deep enough that she'd need stitches, but it wasn't life-threatening. Unlike those shots.

"What happened?" Leigh pressed, still glancing around and no doubt keeping an eye out for the gunman. "Why were you in the woods?"

Kali sobbed, throwing herself against Cullen again. Her face landed against his shoulder. "Someone was breaking in through the front door so I ran out the back."

"But the back door was locked when we got here," Cullen pointed out.

"It locks automatically unless you adjust the thumb turn. And I didn't. I just ran and kept running so I could hide in the trees, but I didn't have my phone with me so I couldn't call anybody."

"Kali, are you all right?" Austin tried again.

"Make him leave," Kali snapped.

Cullen gave Austin a hard stare, hoping that he wouldn't give them any trouble about this.

"She needs to go to the hospital," Austin

insisted, but he turned and headed toward the house.

"I'll have to question you later," Karen called out to him. "And question you, too," she added to Kali. "But Austin's right about you needing to go to the hospital. You should have someone take a look at that cut."

Kali turned not to Karen but to Leigh. "But what if the killer comes back?"

Leigh met her eye to eye. "You saw the killer?"

"No, but he shot at me." Kali paused, then shook her head again. "At least I think he was shooting at me. I didn't see him though."

Hell. Cullen had hoped Kali had at least gotten a glimpse of him. That could have put an end to the danger if they'd gotten an ID. But maybe the CSIs would be able to find something.

Karen stepped to the side to call in the shooting. It didn't take long, and when she was finished, she looked at Leigh. "Two other deputies are on the way here now so they can search the woods." Glancing up at the sun that would be setting in the next hour or so, she added, "A thorough search might have to wait until morning though."

That meant valuable trace could be lost, and

it would sure as heck give the shooter plenty of time to get away.

"I'll go ahead and take Kali into the ER and get her statement," Karen continued a moment later. "I'll send you a copy. Cash will also need statements from Cullen and you."

"I'll make sure he gets them," Leigh told her. "I'd also like to see reports on any evidence the CSIs collect."

"Will do," Karen assured her, and she led Kali away while she kept watch around them.

Cullen and Leigh kept watch as well, but they didn't speak until they were in his truck. "Austin could have been the one to fire those shots," Leigh said.

Since Cullen had already considered the same thing, he nodded. "Or Kali could have."

Leigh's sound of agreement was fast and firm, causing Cullen to curse. Not because he was upset with her but because Kali and Austin had been his friends, and now he wasn't sure if one of them was a killer.

"Rocky could have gotten out here, too. I didn't see anyone following us, but it's possible he overheard us at the town hall."

Definitely possible, and he could have arrived after them and slipped into the woods. He would have had plenty of time to set up a shooting while Leigh and he had been searching inside Kali's house.

But Rocky couldn't have been responsible for the blood drops on the porch.

No. Not enough time for that so maybe Rocky had an accomplice.

Leigh took out her phone, probably to start the calls and texts that a sheriff needed to make when she'd just been under attack, but she stared at the screen a moment and put it away. That's when Cullen noticed that her hands were trembling a little.

"I don't want to go back to the office," she murmured. "I don't want my deputies to see me like this."

It didn't surprise him that she'd held things together while she'd been talking to Kali. That was the job for Leigh. But with the pressure she had coming at her from all sides, she wouldn't want anyone to think she was weak. And Leigh would definitely see trembling hands as weak.

Since his own house still hadn't been cleared by the CSIs, Cullen drove her home, and he hoped like the devil that they wouldn't have any visitors. Leigh didn't need another round with Austin, Rocky or Jeb tonight. Didn't need to tangle with him, either, and that's why he'd give her some space so that maybe she'd be able to get some sleep.

Leigh kept her eyes open, still watching for the gunman, but she lay her head back against the seat. Not relaxing. No. She'd balled her trembling hands into fists, and she was no doubt reliving each and every one of the bullets that'd come at them.

"Rocky's not that good of a shot," she said, getting his attention. "He barely qualifies at the shooting range when he has to take his annual test. What about Austin? Is he into guns?"

Cullen sighed, wishing that she'd been able to turn off her mind at least for this short drive but apparently not. Besides, it was a darn good question.

"Austin collects guns," Cullen explained. "I've never seen him fire one, but people who collect usually know how to use them. That doesn't mean that he's a good shot though."

She made a sound of agreement. "And Kali? I didn't see any guns in her house."

"Don't have a clue if she can shoot or not. But her father is a rancher so she's probably been around firearms." He paused. "Will your brother have Kali and Austin tested for gunshot residue?"

"Probably, but GSR doesn't always show up. And these shots likely came from a rifle so there might not be any GSR on their clothes."

So, it could be another dead end, but at this

point any and all evidence could fall into that category.

Cullen pulled to a stop in front of Leigh's house, and he was pleased when exterior security lights flared on. It made it much easier for them to see that her yard was empty. Still, Cullen didn't take any chances.

When they went inside, they both shed their coats and checked to make sure no one had gotten in. The place was just as they'd left it to go to the meeting at the town hall.

Leigh used her phone to reset the security system, and then she just stood there in the hall. She did the same when her phone rang. She stared at the screen as if debating if she should answer it. Groaning softly, she finally hit the answer button and put the call on speaker.

"Jeb," she said. "What do you want?"

"I want to make sure you're okay and that you're not alone."

She took a couple of moments before she responded. "Cullen's here. He's staying the night again."

Cullen figured that would earn her a lecture from Jeb, but it didn't. "Good," Jeb said. "Because it's not a good idea for you not to have some backup."

"Backup," she repeated. There was both

weariness and a little surprise in her tone. "So, you no longer believe I should be arresting him?"

"No." Jeb paused, sighed. "I heard about the shooting. Heard, too, that Cullen was with you again. If he was behind these attacks, he wouldn't keep putting himself in the line of fire like that."

Leigh sighed as well. "He's not behind the attacks nor the murders. You might have put him in the same tainted light as Bowen, but Cullen's not—"

"I did do that," Jeb admitted. "And I'm sorry."

Leigh pulled back her shoulders. Cullen had a similar reaction because Jeb was not the sort of man to admit a mistake. Worse, this conversation was starting to sound like a last-ditch effort to mend the rift between Leigh and him.

"What's wrong?" Leigh demanded. "Are you sick?"

Jeb's laugh was quick and dry. "I don't have to be sick to tell you that you were right about Cullen. Right about the way you've handled the investigation. Right about a lot of things," he added in a mutter.

"Am I right about you being sick?" she asked.

Jeb's silence confirmed that she was. "I'm

waiting on test results, but the docs think it's my heart. Might need bypass. Might need something more. I won't know for a couple more days, and I hadn't planned on telling you until I knew for sure."

Leigh drew in a long, slow breath. "Does Cash know?"

"No. He doesn't take my calls. And before you say anything, I know he's got reasons for that. So do you. But thanks for hearing me out. If you want, I'll tell you the test results when I have them."

"I want that," she assured him.

It seemed to Cullen that Jeb blew out a sigh of relief. "Good night, Leigh," he added and ended the call.

Once again, Leigh just stood there, but she looked even more exhausted than she had been before Jeb's call.

"I'm sorry," Cullen told her.

She nodded, put her phone away and then turned to him. Their eyes met. Held.

"Don't sleep in the guest room tonight," she whispered, taking hold of his hand. "Come to bed with me."

LEIGH FIGURED SHE should just tell Cullen this was a mistake. Maybe then he'd do the right thing and back away from her.

She knew for a fact that she wouldn't be doing the backing away.

This was despite the lecture she'd given herself about waiting until after the investigation to get involved with him. She should wait. But the fear and emotions were crushing her like an avalanche, and Cullen was the one person who could make that stop. For a little while, anyway.

"The timing for this isn't good," Cullen said. "You want to talk about Jeb?"

Leigh didn't have to take time to consider her answer. "No. I don't want to talk about anything at all. It doesn't have to be sex tonight…" She groaned, pushed her hair from her face and kept her gaze nailed to his. "Yes, it does."

The corner of his mouth lifted, and she got a flash of that hot smile that had no doubt lured many women to his bed. But tonight she was doing the luring. Leigh rethought that though when Cullen pulled her to him and kissed her.

His kiss was exactly what she needed. She sank into it. Sank into his arms, too. Because, mercy, she needed this.

She needed him.

The years they'd been apart vanished, and it felt as if they'd always been together like this. Always *should* be together. But now wasn't the time for Cullen to hear that or for her to realize it.

Cullen picked up on her need for him by her deepening the kiss, and he didn't waste any time backing her into her bedroom. They moved together without breaking the kiss or the arms she'd locked around him.

"I should give you a chance to reconsider," he said, getting off her boots before easing her back on the bed. He looked down at her. "Don't reconsider."

Now it was her turn to smile, and Leigh pulled him down on top of her. All in all, it was a great place for him to be. The weight of his body on hers only fueled this ache she had for him. The kisses did as well when Cullen took his mouth to her neck.

She remembered this part. The foreplay and fire. The urgent heat that started to build inside her. Cullen was very good at the building. At making her need him more than her next breath.

He did something about her breath. He made it vanish when he lowered the kisses to her stomach. He shoved up her top, his mouth teasing her bare skin and kicking up the urgency even more.

Leigh reached for his shirt, but he pinned her hands to the bed and kept on kissing her.

Going lower until he reached the zipper of her jeans. With his own hands locked with hers, he simply used his mouth. And his breath. Cullen kissed her through the denim and kept kissing her until Leigh could take no more.

She rolled with him, reversing their positions so she could go after his shirt. She wanted her mouth on his chest. Wanted to touch him. And she did both. She took a moment to admire the view—the man was built—but she couldn't stave off Cullen.

Once she had his shirt off, he did another flip, straddling her so he could rid her of her shirt. He flicked open her front-hook bra and gave her a quick reminder that breast kisses were hot spots for her. He fanned the heat even higher, managing to kiss one breast, then the other, before he moved lower to shimmy her out of her jeans and panties. He kicked off his own boots as well.

Then, he kept kissing her.

Leigh had no choice but to hang on and enjoy the ride. She fisted her hands on the quilt, anchoring herself, but she knew that if he kept up those clever flicks of his tongue that she'd climax too fast.

"We do this together," she insisted.

She maneuvered away from him so that she could tackle his jeans. And finally his boxers.

Yes, the man was built, and the past decade had only improved everything about him.

"Condom," he ground out when she ran her hand the long length of him. "In my wallet."

Since she wanted that long length inside her, Leigh rummaged through his jeans, located the wallet, then the condom.

Cullen did some more maneuvering, flipping their positions again so that he was on top of her. Thankfully, it didn't take him long to get the condom on, and with their gazes locked, he slipped inside her.

The pleasure speared through her, and the sound she made was a long, slow moan. It felt as if she'd been waiting for this for way too long.

Cullen made his own sound of pleasure, and he began to move inside her. Building the fire with each maddening stroke. Making everything pinpoint to the need to finish this. And that's what he did.

He finished it.

Leigh held on to Cullen and let him finish her.

Chapter Fourteen

Cullen sipped his coffee while he stared out Leigh's kitchen window. It was a good view of the frost-covered pastures, the barn and the horses.

Leigh had set up automatic feed dispensers, probably because of the long hours she often worked, and he'd heard talk that she had part-time help for the chores that came with running a small horse ranch. But for this morning, they had the place to themselves.

That's why he'd found it damn hard to leave her bed.

However, Cullen had forced himself away from her and into the shower. Then, into the kitchen so he could give her some thinking time. He fully expected when she came to her senses that she'd tell him they'd made a huge mistake by having sex. And maybe they had. But at the moment it felt like something he wanted to continue doing beyond just this time together. First though, they had to find a killer and stop him or her from coming after them again.

He continued to sip coffee, and then saw Leigh. Not in the house but headed toward the pasture. Since she hadn't come through the kitchen, she'd likely gone out through the patio doors off her bedroom.

Wearing a bulky buckskin work coat, she stopped at the pasture fence, and a bay mare immediately came to her. Leigh ran her hand over the horse and murmured something. Even though Cullen couldn't hear what she said, he smiled. Obviously, they had common ground when it came to their love of horses.

His smile faded though when he remembered that it wasn't a good idea for her to be out in the open like that. Not with a killer on the loose. A killer who favored taking shots at them. Cullen grabbed his coat and went to join her.

The sun was out, making everything look as if it'd been doused with diamond dust, but the cold air still had a sting to it. His boots crunched on the ice-crusted grass, and it was that sound that likely alerted her, because with her hand still stroking the mare, Leigh turned to look at him.

"I know," she said before he could speak.

"I shouldn't be out here. But being around the horses helps me clear my mind."

He smiled again. Yeah, they had common ground all right.

"This is Buttercup," Leigh said, introducing him to the mare. "And that's Smoky and Honey." She tipped her head to two other horses, who were also heading their way. "If they'd caught a stranger's scent, they would let me know about it. Like now." All three horses were snorting and whinnying.

Well, they weren't as good as guard dogs in sending up an alarm, but it was better than nothing.

Because he wanted the taste of her, Cullen moved closer and brushed his mouth over hers. That also got him some attention from the mare, who gave his arm a nudge. He gave her a quick rub, then lingered a moment longer on the kiss with Leigh.

Leigh eased back, her eyes partly closed and a dreamy look on her face. Obviously, the kiss had been just as potent for her as it was for him. But potency aside, being out here was too dangerous. Cullen hooked his arm around Leigh to lead her back to the house. He considered trying to coax her to bed, but they'd barely made it inside the kitchen when her phone rang.

"It's Vance," she said, answering and putting the call on speaker.

Since this almost certainly had something to do with the investigation, Cullen was very interested in what the deputy had to say.

"Just got off the phone with the crime lab," Vance explained. "It's not good news. The fingerprint on the SUV is too smudged for them to get a match."

Leigh didn't groan, probably because she'd already considered that might be the outcome. She shucked off her coat and put it on the peg by the door. Cullen did the same.

"I want you to put out the word that the print isn't smudged and that the crime lab believes they'll be able to get a match from the database," she told Vance after a short pause. "Tell everyone you know because I want word to get back to the killer. But also alert the lab so they've got full security in place in case the killer tries to eliminate the evidence."

"Will do," Vance assured her.

Cullen could help with that, too, and he fired off a quick text to Austin. He told Austin that it was good news, that the killer might soon be ID'd. If Austin was guilty and did indeed try to destroy evidence against him, then he'd be caught. That still felt like a heavyweight's punch, but it was better than having Austin come after Leigh.

"I'll be in the office soon," Leigh added to Vance a moment later. She ended the call, but before she could put her phone away, it rang again.

"Cash," she said, glancing at the screen. The muscles stirred in her jaw. "I'm not going to tell him about Jeb. Not over the phone. I'll pay him a visit to give him the news."

That made sense, and her tone let Cullen know that her father's illness was weighing on her. Despite the rift between them, she almost certainly still loved him.

As she'd done with Vance, Leigh put the call on speaker while she helped herself to a cup of coffee. "Please tell me you found the shooter," Leigh greeted her brother.

"No," Cash answered after a huff. "And I'm about to add another complication to your murder investigation."

"What happened?" Leigh demanded.

"I'd better start with what didn't happen," Cash explained. "Kali didn't have a break-in, and she didn't run into the woods because she was afraid. During the interview, she broke down and admitted that it was all staged. She claimed she knew Austin was coming over because he'd texted her and said he was. So, she told me that she set up her injury to leave the blood drops, and then she ran and hid so it'd make him sick with worry."

Leigh groaned and set her coffee aside so she could scrub her hands over her face. "And what about the shooter?"

"Kali insists she doesn't have a clue about that. Says she didn't see anyone in the woods before or after the shots started."

"You believe her?" Leigh pressed.

This time Cash wasn't so fast to answer. "Not sure. Plenty of people are good liars, and I don't know if she's one of them. But if she fired those shots, then the rifle is probably still somewhere in the woods, and the CSIs are out looking for it now."

Leigh gathered her breath before she spoke again. "Did Kali agree to let you test for GSR?"

"She did. Nada. Then again, the EMTs had their hands all over her clothes when they examined her. She had a panic attack in the ambulance, and they had to restrain her."

Cullen didn't even bother to curse. Leigh had already known that the GSR would be a long shot.

"Unless I can prove Kali's the shooter," Cash went on, "I can't charge her with anything other than a misdemeanor for wasting law enforcement resources. She didn't make a false 911 call, and she admitted the ruse once I got her in interview. I can't arrest her for wanting to worry her ex-boyfriend."

No, but it did show how desperate and hurt Kali was. So desperate and so hurt that she might have killed Alexa. Especially if Alexa had taunted Kali about her affair with Austin.

Leigh finished her call with her brother, gulped down some more coffee and gave her shoulder harness an adjustment. "You should be able to go back to the Triple R sometime this morning," she said, her gaze lifting to meet his. "But you're welcome to stay here."

That was an invitation Cullen had no intention of turning down. Not just because he wanted to be with Leigh but also because he wasn't about to leave her alone as long as the killer was still gunning for them. Cullen would have told her that, too, but they got another call. This time, it was his phone.

"It's Jamie," he said, answering right away. He also put it on speaker. "Are you okay?" Cullen immediately asked him.

Jamie, however, didn't give him an immediate answer. "I'm getting out of the hospital. Deputy Cecile Taggart is still here, and she's going to drive me to the bunkhouse."

Cullen was thankful Jamie would still have police protection, but something was wrong.

He didn't think he was mistaken about the worry he'd heard in Jamie's voice.

"Did something happen?" Cullen came out and asked.

"Yeah. And that's why I need to talk to the sheriff and you." Again, Jamie hesitated, and he lowered his voice to a whisper. "The killer called me again."

LEIGH RESISTED SNATCHING the phone right out of Cullen's hand, but she did hurry to get closer so that Jamie would have no trouble hearing her. "What did the killer say to you?" she demanded.

"I don't want to get into it here over the phone," Jamie said, still hesitating, still whispering. "Deputy Taggart and I will be at your house soon. I need to talk to you about going into protective custody or something. I can't go on like this."

Jamie hung up before she could demand again that he tell her about the phone call he'd gotten from the killer.

"I should go to the hospital," Leigh grumbled.

"You could end up passing him and Cecile on the road," Cullen quickly pointed out.

His voice was calm and reasonable. Too bad she wasn't feeling either at the moment. She wanted to know about the killer, and Jamie might have key information. Information that could possibly stop another attack.

"Witness protection," she repeated like profanity. "I'm guessing that means the killer threatened him again." And that reminder sent some fresh alarm through her. "I should send Cecile backup."

She whipped out her phone and called the deputy, and Cecile must have been expecting her call, because she answered on the first ring.

"Jamie's fine," Cecile said right off. "He's just scared. We're heading out of the hospital right now, and then I'll drive him straight to your place."

"Why is he scared? What did the killer tell him?" Leigh pressed.

"I don't know. I didn't hear any of the actual call, but he's insisting on talking to you about it. I called your office and they said you were still home so I figured that's where I'd bring him. I had Dawn come here to the hospital, too, so she'll ride along with us."

Some of the tightness eased in Leigh's chest. She had good cops working for her, and this was proof of it. Cecile had arranged for backup on her own. Maybe it wouldn't be necessary, but taking precautions was the right call.

"Come straight here," Leigh instructed. "If

we end up doing protective custody, I've got contacts with the marshals that I can bring in. That way, they could meet with Jamie here so he doesn't have to go back out again."

"Will do," Cecile assured her. "We're getting in the cruiser right now and will be there in just a couple of minutes," she added before she ended the call.

"I can arrange for security at the ranch, too, if Jamie wants to go back to the bunkhouse," Cullen offered. "Or if he wants to go to his folks' place, I can send men there with him."

Leigh gave his arm a gentle squeeze. "Thank you." She took a deep breath. "I just wish I knew if Jamie was in actual danger or if the killer is just trying to intimidate him. Either way, he needs protection," she added in a mumble.

"Nick might be able to help," Cullen suggested.

It'd been a while since she'd seen his brother, but since Nick was an ATF agent, it was highly likely that he had other contacts in law enforcement. Nick might be able to streamline the process for Jamie.

When she heard the sound of an engine approaching the house, Cullen and she hurried to the front window. But it wasn't a police cruiser. It was a big silver four-by-four truck that maneuvered over the dirt and gravel like a bulldozer, and it pulled to a stop behind Cullen's truck.

Cullen groaned. "It's Bowen."

Leigh wanted to groan as well. She didn't have time for a visit from a man who was likely there to give her grief.

She disarmed the security system so Cullen could open the front door, and Leigh went onto the porch with him when he faced down his father. Bowen stepped from his truck, leaving the engine running and door open as he started toward them. He sighed in obvious disapproval when he saw them.

"It's true, then," Bowen said to Cullen. He stopped at the bottom porch step and stared up at them. A stare from narrowed eyes. "You're staying here with Leigh."

Yep, she'd been right about the grief-giving, and apparently Bowen was going to dole some of it out to Cullen as well as her.

"Last I heard I didn't have to check with you about my sleeping arrangements," Cullen fired back.

"Well, you should because you know Jeb will use this to try to lock you up." Bowen flung his index finger at Leigh. "And she might not be able to save you. They're trying to kick her out of office."

"Yes," Cullen agreed, "and they're trying that because she won't give in to the gossip that I killed Alexa." He put his hands on his hips, shook his head. "You and Jeb are a lot alike, you know. He was at the station and had the same complaint."

"Of course he did," Bowen snarled. "He'd rather see you dead than with his daughter."

That might be true, but Leigh didn't believe Jeb would do anything to cause Cullen's demise. However, Jeb might indeed want to rid her of her badge so she couldn't tarnish the reputation he had in the county.

"I'm pretty sure I'm in love with Leigh," Cullen said, stunning his father.

However, Bowen's reaction was a drop in the bucket compared to Leigh's. "What?" she managed to say.

Cullen had likely tossed that out in anger. Something to get his father off his back. But one look at him, and Leigh thought it might be true.

Well, heck.

This wasn't good. Not now, anyway. She didn't have the focus or time to sort out how she felt about that announcement. Or how she felt about Cullen for that matter. Yes, she had feelings for him. Deep ones. Always had. But love? It was something she had to push to the back of her mind though because the cruiser pulled into the driveway. Dawn was behind the wheel, and she pulled up in front of Bowen's truck.

"This conversation isn't over," Bowen said like a warning. "I'll come back after you've dealt with business."

"Just stay put a couple more seconds," Leigh instructed, keeping her attention on the cruiser. "You can leave after Jamie's inside the house."

"Jamie?" Bowen asked, and there seemed to be genuine concern in his voice. "What's he doing here?'"

"Business," Leigh said, using Bowen's own choice of words.

The young ranch hand got out from the back seat of the cruiser. There was a white bandage on his head, and he looked more than a little pale and wobbly. The unsteadiness was probably why Cecile rushed around the cruiser to take hold of Jamie's arm. Leigh went into the yard, too, with Cullen right behind her. Something Leigh appreciated. If Jamie was about to collapse, they might need Cullen's muscle to get him into the house.

Leigh intended to call the doctor as soon as Jamie was safe. No way did he look ready to have been released from the hospital. Then again, maybe Jamie had pushed for his release because he'd been afraid the killer would get to him.

With Cullen on one side of Jamie and Cecile on the other, they started toward the house.

"Is the boy all right?" Bowen asked.

Leigh was asking herself the same thing. But she didn't get a chance to answer Bowen.

Before someone fired a shot.

CULLEN MOVED FAST when he heard the gunshot. He hooked his arm around Leigh's waist and pulled her to the ground next to some shrubs and landscape boulders. Cecile did the same with Jamie. But the deputy wasn't fast enough.

The bullet slammed into her shoulder.

"Cecile," Leigh said on a gasp, and she pulled away from Cullen so she could go to her deputy.

Apparently, Dawn was trying to do the same thing. Cullen heard the cruiser door open. Heard the shot that followed. And because he was on the ground, he could see Dawn fall on the other side of the cruiser.

Hell.

There were two deputies down.

Cecile was alive. Cullen could see that. But he could also see the blood that was already spreading across the front of her coat. Cecile was also writhing in pain. Pain that would get a whole lot worse if the shooter managed to put another bullet in her.

Cullen couldn't see Dawn well enough to know if she was alive, but she wasn't moving. Definitely not a good sign.

"Oh, God," Jamie muttered, and he kept repeating it.

Another shot came, this one slamming into the ground between them and Bowen.

"Get down!" Cullen yelled to his father, and he drew his gun.

But there really wasn't any cover where he was. Ditto for Leigh, Jamie, Cecile and him. They were all literally out in the open in the yard with two injured cops and a ranch hand who looked on the verge of a full-out panic attack.

While Leigh applied pressure to Cecile's wound, Cullen made a quick call to the police station to get them some backup. It wouldn't take long for the other deputies to arrive, but a gunman could take them all out in just a matter of seconds.

Cullen had to do something about that. He couldn't just let Dawn and Cecile bleed out. He glanced around, looking for a way to get everyone to safety. The cruiser was a good fifteen feet away. It was the same for Bowen's truck. They'd be easy targets if they tried to get to them.

Another bullet cracked through the air, and because he'd been waiting for it, Cullen used the sound to pinpoint the location. The shooter was to the right of Leigh's yard, probably in the thick cluster of oak and pecan trees.

"Get flat on the ground next to those bushes and try to crawl to the left side of the house," he told Bowen, but his father was already scrambling to do that.

More shots came, and none seemed to be aimed at Bowen. They all came toward Leigh. Even though Cullen knew she wasn't going to like it, he climbed over her, took aim in the direction of the shooter, and he fired. It didn't faze the shooter one bit because he sent more bullets their way.

Making a sound of outrage, Leigh levered herself up, and she, too, fired at the gunman. Cullen figured the chances of either of them hitting the guy were slim to none, but they needed a lull in the gunfire so they could get to the side of the house where Bowen was.

"I'll get to Bowen's truck," Cullen told Leigh, and he made sure it sounded like a plan of action and not a suggestion. "I'll bring it here so we can get Jamie and Cecile inside."

Leigh was already shaking her head before

he finished. "He'll shoot you before you can get to it."

Maybe. *Probably*, Cullen silently amended. "You can try to take him out when his attention's focused on me."

She was still shaking her head when they heard the sound of more gunfire. But this hadn't come from the direction of the shooter. No. This was coming from the far right, behind Leigh's house. And it wasn't aimed at Leigh and him but rather at the shooter.

"Bowen," Leigh said, glancing in the direction where Cullen had last seen his father. Bowen was no longer there. Since his father always carried a gun, he'd probably gone around the back of the house so he could try to stop the gunman.

And it worked.

Well, it worked in distracting the gunman, anyway, because the shots began to go in Bowen's direction. Cullen knew Bowen was taking a huge risk. One that Cullen hoped didn't cost him his life. But maybe it would be enough of a diversion for him to get Leigh, Jamie and Cecile behind cover.

"Jamie, you need to stay down and move," Cullen told him, and he hoisted Cecile over his shoulder in a fireman's carry. The deputy moaned in pain, but she was still conscious.

Leigh's eyes met Cullen's. It was just a split-second glance, but a lot of things passed between them. The fear. And the hope. This was their chance, and they had to take it.

"We need to get to the left side of the house," Leigh added.

Cullen was right there with her, and once he was sure Jamie was in a crouching position, Cullen got them moving. Leigh turned, covering their backs as they hurried across the stretch of yard.

It didn't take long for the bullets to come their way.

They smacked into the ground, tearing up the grass and dirt. But Bowen didn't let up. He continued to fire shots at the gunman, and Cullen figured that slowed the guy down at least a little.

Each inch across the yard seemed to take an eternity, and with each step, Cullen's heart pounded even harder. His fears skyrocketed. Not for himself. But for Leigh. She was putting herself between them and the shooter. Not only that, she was almost certainly the primary target.

The moment Cullen reached the left side of the house, he caught onto Jamie, dragging him to the ground and handing him Cecile. Thankfully, Jamie took the injured deputy and that

freed up Cullen to lean out and give Leigh and
Bowen some help. He fired at the gunman until
Leigh was able to scramble next to him.

"I need to get some help for Dawn," Leigh
immediately said, taking out her phone.

She called dispatch to request medical assis-
tance, but Cullen tuned her out when he heard
the hurried footsteps coming from the back of
the house. He pivoted in that direction, bringing up his gun, but it wasn't the threat his body
had braced for.

It was Bowen.

His father wasn't hurt, which was somewhat
of a miracle, and with his gun still drawn, he
hurried toward them.

"Who's trying to kill us?" Bowen snarled.

Cullen shook his head and turned back to
the front yard so he could keep watch. He
didn't see the gunman, but he saw something
else. Dawn. The deputy was crawling to the
front of the cruiser. Like Cecile, she was bleeding, but at least she was alive. She might not
be that way for long though if they couldn't
get an ambulance out here.

"I can try to make a run for my truck,"
Bowen said, causing Cullen to glance back
at him.

There were times his father's stubbornness
could irritate the heck out of him, but Bowen

was no coward. He would indeed go out there just as he'd drawn fire so that the rest of them could get to cover.

"There's an ATV in the barn," Leigh said when she finished her call. "One of us could use it to get Cecile to the trail at the back of my property. The trail leads out to the road. She needs to get to the hospital ASAP," she added, looking directly at Cullen.

Cullen had no doubts that Leigh meant for him to be getting Cecile out of there. He wouldn't have minded doing just that if it didn't mean leaving Leigh behind. Where he knew for a fact that she would take huge risks to try to get to Dawn.

"And what about Dawn?" Cullen asked her.

"I can go through the back door into my house. One of the windows on that side should make it easier to take out the shooter."

It would. And Leigh would have the added advantage of having some cover.

"You'll take Cecile to the ATV in the barn?" Cullen asked his father.

Bowen hesitated, but that was probably because he, too, was thinking of the danger to those who stayed behind. His father finally nodded and hoisted Cecile as Cullen had done. "But, damn it, don't do anything stupid."

Cullen didn't make him any promises.

Couldn't. Because he'd definitely do something stupid if it meant keeping Leigh safe. Unfortunately, she probably had the same thing in mind when it came to him.

"I'll be in the house with Leigh," Cullen explained, still keeping watch of the front and back yards. He didn't want the shooter sneaking up on them from behind.

"I can help Mr. Brodie with Cecile," Jamie volunteered. "Then, I can wait in the barn until it's okay to come out."

Leigh nodded. "Let's go."

As she'd done in the yard, Leigh took the back position, and Cullen jogged ahead so he could make sure the gunman wasn't lying in wait for them. He didn't see anyone so he gave Bowen and Jamie the go-ahead to get to the barn. They were only about halfway there when Cullen heard something he definitely hadn't wanted to hear.

Not a gunshot.

But an engine.

It was Bowen's massive truck, and when the driver hit the accelerator, the truck barreled right toward them.

Chapter Fifteen

Leigh got a quick flash of images from when the SUV had rammed into her cruiser. Those had been some terrifying moments, but at least she and Cullen had been in the vehicle. There'd been some protection.

Not now though.

They were out in the open, where they could be mowed down and killed.

"Run!" she shouted.

That order wasn't just to Cullen but to Bowen and Jamie. They weren't in the barn yet, and they were out in the open, too, where they'd be easy targets. Especially since Bowen was carrying Cecile and Jamie obviously wasn't in any shape to outrun a truck with a driver hell-bent on killing them.

Leigh didn't dare take the time to look back to see how close the truck was to them. Every second counted now, and the moment she reached the back porch, she cursed the railing. It was too high to vault over, and if she tried to climb it, she could be sideswiped. That meant going around and up the steps.

But she didn't get a chance to do that.

From the corner of her eye, she saw Jamie fall, but it was just a blur of motion because she was moving. Or rather Cullen was moving her. He caught onto her arm, jerking her away from the porch.

And it wasn't a second too soon.

Because the truck rammed into the exact spot where she'd just been.

Neither Cullen nor she had had time to fire at the driver, but Cullen's momentum got them away from the impact. They fell, but immediately scrambled to get up. However, Jamie wasn't doing the same. He was still down, and Bowen must not have even noticed because he was still barreling toward the barn with Cecile in tow.

The railing on the porch gave way. So did part of the porch. However, the truck didn't seem damaged at all. The driver spun it around, taking aim at Cullen and her again.

Leigh had to make a quick decision. If Cullen and she ran toward Jamie, they might not be able to get him up in time to stop him from being run over. Obviously, Cullen had the same concern because he took hold of her arm and started running toward the front of the house.

Where the cruiser was.

And Dawn.

The truck would almost certainly follow them, but if they could get the deputy into the cruiser, then they stood a chance of protecting her. Then, they could drive back around to the barn to help Jamie and Bowen.

Leigh braced herself in case someone fired shots at them. After all, the driver could be working with a partner. But the only threat came from the truck itself. The driver managed to get it turned around and came at Cullen and her again when they reached the front yard. Because the windshield was so heavily tinted, they couldn't see who was trying to kill them.

Once again, Cullen and she had to dive out of the way of the speeding truck. It whipped right past them, so close that Leigh could feel the heat of the engine. They fell again. Hard. Leigh rammed into some rocks, causing the pain to shoot through her. The impact also knocked the breath out of her, and she lost critical moments of time fighting for air. No way could she stand when she couldn't breathe.

Cullen helped with that though. He got to his feet, hauling her up and practically dragging her out of the way. Good thing, too. Because the driver threw the truck into Reverse and came at them again.

Leigh was thankful that Cullen still had hold of her because he got them out of the way again, this time diving behind some landscape boulders. Still, they'd just come close to dying, and it was obvious the driver wasn't finished. He did a doughnut in the yard, the tires slinging up dirt and rocks. Obviously, taking aim at them again.

But he didn't hit the accelerator.

He just sat there, revving the engine. Waiting. But for what? Maybe he thought it would shred the tires if he hit the boulders. And it might. But the two-foot-high rocks wouldn't give them enough protection if he started shooting. That's why Leigh had to try to stop him from doing that. She still had hold of her gun so she pointed it at the windshield.

And she fired.

Just as the driver sped forward. Her bullet tore through the safety glass, and she cursed when she realized her shot had been off. Not directly at the driver but a little to the left. She might have injured him, but it likely hadn't been a headshot. Right now, she figured killing him was the only way for the rest of them to survive. If this killer managed to take out

Cullen and her, he'd take out the rest. No way would he want to leave witnesses behind.

Cullen pulled her to her feet again, and they darted to the left. But not far. The driver would have to at least clip the boulders to get to them. That would certainly slow him down.

However, he didn't come at them again.

The driver spun around, speeding not toward them but rather in the direction of the barn. Leigh's stomach went to her knees because she was pretty sure she knew what he was doing. He was going after Jamie, Bowen and Cecile.

"No!" Leigh shouted, hoping to draw the driver's attention.

But she didn't. The truck kept going, past the house and into the backyard. Straight to Jamie. He was still on the ground, but he was conscious, because he was struggling to get up and out of the way.

With the howl of police and ambulance sirens just up the road, Cullen and she started running. Hoping to stop the driver from killing the ranch hand. However, there was a lot of distance between Jamie and them.

The driver slammed on the brakes, but Leigh couldn't tell if he'd hit Jamie or not. She couldn't tell if Jamie was still alive. Worse, she couldn't see the driver. But she heard what she thought was the passenger's-side door opening.

"He's grabbing Jamie," Cullen said, pulling up so he could take aim.

Leigh immediately understood why he'd do that. The killer had to know backup was on the way, and he could use Jamie to escape. But there was a possibility that was much worse. Maybe he was about to kill Jamie so he could eliminate him as a loose end.

"I can't risk shooting," Cullen snarled like profanity.

No, he couldn't. Because he might hit Jamie instead. The windshield wouldn't help with that, either. There was a gaping hole from her own shot, but the rest of the glass had cracked and webbed. It was as effective as putting a mask on the killer.

She heard the door slam, and the driver quickly turned the truck around. So that it was facing Cullen and her again. It came at them. Slowly this time. Like a predator stalking its prey. Since that slow pace could mean the driver was preparing to fire at them, Cullen and she moved back behind the boulders. Even if they were belly-down, it wouldn't stop them from being shot, but it was better than standing out in the open with a killer bearing down on them.

"Be ready to jump out of the way," Leigh warned Cullen.

The driver held the snail-crawling pace until he stopped just a few yards away from them. Leigh saw some movement behind the damaged glass, and a moment later, Jamie peered through the fist-sized hole in the windshield. She could only see part of his face, but it was enough for her to know he was terrified.

"Me for you," Jamie said, his voice trembling with fear. He aimed those fear-filled eyes at Leigh. "That's the deal I'm supposed to tell you. If you don't trade places with me, I'll die."

HELL. THAT WAS the one word that kept going through Cullen's mind.

It was bad enough that Leigh and he had to face down a killer, but now Jamie was in the middle of it.

Cullen seriously doubted that Jamie was in any shape to fight off the killer, especially since he was almost certainly being held at gunpoint. Being told what to say, too. The killer had no doubt told Jamie word for word what he was supposed to say to Leigh and him.

He made a quick glance at the road and spotted a cruiser and an ambulance. They'd turned off their sirens, but their lights were still flaring. Leigh obviously saw them, too, and she fired off a text. "I told Vance to try to get Dawn out of here and take her to the EMTs," she relayed to Cullen. "I don't want him or the ambulance coming any closer."

That was a wise decision. If the cruiser came speeding in, it might help Leigh and him by giving them some cover, but it could be a deadly move for Jamie. If the killer didn't shoot him on the spot, he might try to flee with him. Then, the snake could just murder Jamie once he was in the clear.

But Cullen wanted to make sure this SOB didn't get away.

"Me for you," Jamie repeated.

"And how do I know you won't gun all three of us down if we make this trade?" Leigh called out to the driver.

There was a short silence, probably for Jamie to get his instructions, and he finally said, "You don't know. It's a risk you'll have to take if you want to keep me alive." Jamie's voice trembled. Then, it broke. "Don't take the risk," he blurted out. "Don't trade yourselves for me."

Cullen could see enough of Jamie to spot the barrel of a gun as it jammed into the ranch hand's temple.

"All of this is to cover up you murdering Alexa," Leigh called out. "And it's stupid.

Backup's already arrived, and you won't be able to get out of here. Just toss down your weapon, let Jamie go, and I'll see what kind of deal I can work out."

Jamie winced when the gun dug even harder into his head, but he didn't say anything for several seconds. "You're lying. There'll be no deal," he said, obviously repeating what the killer had told him.

The killer was right about that. No way would he get a reduced sentence when he'd murdered at least two people and attempted to murder others, including cops. Still, maybe there was a way to bargain with him.

Or her.

Cullen couldn't rule out that it was Kali behind the wheel. It wouldn't have taken much muscle to force Jamie into the truck at gunpoint.

"If your plan is to get away, you'll need money," Cullen called out to the killer. "You could consider it a ransom. I'll pay you to release Jamie."

"Money won't fix this," Jamie said, repeating his instructions. "But Leigh and you will. This is your last chance," Jamie added. "Me for you."

"Any chance you have a shot?" Leigh asked him.

Cullen studied the distorted images behind

the heavily tinted glass. "Maybe. I figure the killer is still behind the wheel. Maybe keeping low. But I could keep the shot to the side so that it won't hit Jamie."

Well, maybe it wouldn't. Cullen doubted the driver had Jamie fully in front of him like a human shield—there wouldn't be enough room for that—but any shot would be a risk. If Cullen didn't kill the driver, then he or she could turn the gun on Jamie. Of course, the odds of that happening were already sky-high.

That's why they had to go for it.

"I'll take the shot," Cullen told her.

She nodded, her breath mixing with the cold air and creating a wispy fog between them. "On the count of three, you fire, and I'll run to the side of the house. That might buy Jamie some time."

Yeah, it would. Because the killer would turn the gun on Leigh.

"No." Cullen couldn't say that fast enough. "You're not running out there."

Leigh looked him straight in the eyes. "Neither one of us can crouch here and let Jamie die. It's what has to be done."

Cullen cursed, ready to argue with her, but then he spotted something he definitely hadn't wanted to see.

Bowen.

Crouched down, his father had come out of the barn, and it was obvious he was trying to sneak up on the driver of the truck. Not directly behind it. But rather to the side. It'd be a damn good way for Bowen to get himself killed.

"What the heck is he doing?" Leigh snarled. "Text him. Tell him to get down right now."

Even if Bowen read the text, he wouldn't just get down. His father's stubborn streak wasn't reserved just for Jeb and members of his family. However, Cullen had to try, and he motioned for Bowen to drop.

He didn't.

Bowen took aim at the back tires of the truck, and he started firing. Not one shot but a barrage of them that would almost certainly flatten the tires and prevent a quick escape. But it wasn't escape that Cullen was immediately worried about. It was Bowen and Jamie.

The driver's-side door flew open, and Cullen saw Jamie being dragged out of the vehicle. Now he was a human shield, and that position prevented Cullen from seeing who was holding him, especially since his captor was hunkering down.

"Keep that up, and I die," Jamie yelled.

Again, it was the words the killer wanted him to say, and Cullen was thankful he could actually say them. Because it meant he was still alive. The killer hadn't panicked and just taken him out.

Not yet, anyway.

However, the fact that Jamie was being forced to do all the talking meant the killer didn't want Cullen or Leigh to hear his or her voice because they would recognize who it was.

Bowen did stop firing, and he had the sense to drop down on the ground. That, and the fact that he was on the other side of the truck from the killer, might prevent him from being shot.

Leigh levered herself up a little and took aim. Cullen had to resist the need to push her back down. To give her that small margin of cover. But she was a cop, and no way would she put her safety over Jamie's.

"Bring the cruiser around to the back," Jamie said.

So, the killer wasn't panicking or giving up. He could use the cruiser to escape, and if he managed that, then Leigh wouldn't be safe. This snake would just keep coming after her.

"I'm going to take that shot now," Cullen whispered to Leigh. "I'll aim for their legs. If I miss and shoot Jamie, he'll drop down. That'll give you a clearer shot at the killer."

She pulled her gaze from the truck for just

a second, and in that quick flash of time, he could see her trying to work out whether or not that was the right thing to do. It might or might not be. Cullen knew that. And so did she. But they had to do something before this escalated even more.

"The cruiser now," Jamie shouted. "You've got one minute."

Leigh nodded. "Take the shot," she told Cullen.

She got into a crouch, and he knew what she had in mind. She was going to make that run to the side of her house to create a distraction. And to get herself in a better position to take a kill shot. Again, he had to do battle with his instincts to try to keep her safe. Instead, he brushed a quick kiss on her mouth and took aim.

"Now," Cullen said.

And Leigh took off running.

Cullen kept the shot low, going for the edge of the boot that he saw behind Jamie's, and he pulled the trigger. The shot blasted through the air. So did the howl of pain.

A man's howl.

Bowen lifted his head and his gun, trying to take aim. The killer shifted, staggering a little. Enough to let Cullen know that he'd hit his target. But the killer quickly recovered. At the exact moment Leigh reached the side of her house, the killer pivoted, hooking his arm around Jamie's neck and dragging his human shield back in front of him.

"Big mistake," the killer yelled. "Now Jamie dies."

The words were like fists, but Cullen now knew exactly who they were dealing with because he had no trouble recognizing the voice.

Rocky was the killer.

LEIGH HAD KNOWN that it could be Rocky behind the wheel of the truck. But it still brought on an avalanche of emotions. Anger, betrayal, shock. He'd worked side by side with her, and until the last twenty-four hours, she hadn't seen any signs that he was a killer.

But she was seeing them now.

Rocky had a gun to Jamie's head, and Leigh knew with absolute certainty that he'd kill Jamie. In fact, the only reason Rocky hadn't already pulled the trigger was because he needed a shield, and the terrified Jamie was it. However, it wasn't Jamie Rocky wanted.

No.

He wanted her. Probably Cullen, too, but Leigh wasn't sure she knew the reason for that.

"Have you always wanted me dead?" Leigh called out to him. "Or were you worried I'd prove that you're the one who murdered Alexa and McNash?"

"You don't deserve the badge," Rocky spat out.

His response surprised her. Not because of his obvious venom, but because he'd answered her at all. Leigh had figured he'd just spout out his demand for the cruiser so he could make his escape.

Something she wanted to make sure didn't happen.

That's why Leigh glanced around to try to figure out how to stop him. Rocky was going to pay for the murders—which he hadn't denied. Pay for the attacks against Cullen and her, too. And he was especially going to pay for the hell he was putting Jamie through.

From the angle she had now, she could no longer see Bowen, but it was possible he'd try to sneak up on Rocky. Which wouldn't be a good thing. It could cause Rocky to have a knee-jerk reaction and pull the trigger. Especially since Rocky was already hurt. There was blood on his leg just above his boot.

Cullen was still on the ground, using the boulders for cover, but he also had his gun aimed and ready. If he got a shot, she could count on him to take it—and not miss.

She didn't know where Vance was but suspected the text she'd just gotten was from him. Probably asking for instructions on what he should do. Without taking her attention, or her aim, off Rocky, Leigh motioned toward the last spot where she'd seen Dawn. If Vance hadn't gotten to her already, then maybe he'd do that now.

The one person Leigh didn't want to look at was Jamie. She could practically feel the fear coming off him in hot, slick waves, and she couldn't let her worry for him get in the way. He could help best by diffusing this mess.

"So, you wanted me dead because I'm the sheriff," Leigh called out to Rocky.

"You're sleeping with Cullen Brodie," Rocky snapped. "Now, quit yapping and get me that cruiser." He peppered that *request* with a lot of crude profanity.

Again, she wasn't surprised that Rocky was enraged about her relationship with Cullen. With a Brodie. Jeb's anger toward Bowen might not have erupted into violence, but it had spilled over to Rocky. Still, she wasn't putting a drop of the blame on Jeb. This was Rocky's deal, and she was betting at the core that it had less to do with his feelings about Cullen than it did about him trying to cover up Alexa's murder.

And she'd try to use that.

"You killed Alexa in the heat of the moment," Leigh said, trying to keep her voice calm. "That's second-degree murder. Maybe even manslaughter."

Rocky gave a hollow laugh. "You expect me to believe you'd offer me a deal! Don't insult me. I'm a cop. A better cop than you'll ever be."

She could have pointed out that he was a killer and had also committed numerous other felonies, but that wouldn't help diffuse this. Maybe nothing would help, but she had to try for Jamie's sake.

"Maybe you are a better cop," she said. "Because I can't figure out why you'd kill Alexa."

"No more yapping," he yelled. "Get me that cruiser now."

"It'll take a couple of minutes. Vance used it to get Dawn to the ambulance. She's hurt, Rocky, and she needs the EMTs so she won't bleed out."

Rocky cursed. "She got in the way. She got herself shot. Like Alexa."

Wincing, Rocky staggered back a step. Obviously, the gunshot wound was giving him some pain, and pain didn't go well with logical thought.

"The cruiser," Rocky shouted. "Get it now, or I'll start putting bullets in Jamie. While I'm at it, I'll send some shots at Cullen and you. I might get real lucky and finish you both off."

Even with Rocky's stagger, Cullen still didn't have a shot so Leigh sent a quick text to Vance to have him bring the cruiser around. She had no intention of letting Rocky get in with Jamie, but with all the maneuvering around that would take, it would increase their chances of one of them getting that clean shot.

She heard the movement behind her and thought it was Vance. Still, she pivoted in case Rocky was working with a partner. So did Cullen. And they saw Jeb walking toward them.

"Get back," Leigh warned him.

But Jeb kept on walking, and he wasn't using anything for cover. He was out in the open, and he had his hands lifted, maybe in surrender, maybe to show Rocky he wasn't armed.

"You don't want to do this, Rocky," Jeb said, his voice as calm as a lake. "You're scaring the boy. Let Jamie go, and we can talk this out."

"I got no choice," Rocky argued. "You understand that." There was nothing calm about his voice. Every word had a sharp, raw edge to it.

Leigh wanted to curse her father for doing this. For putting himself in the direct line of fire. But if she went into the yard to drag him back, it could get them both killed.

"I understand. But you've got choices," Jeb argued back. "You can drop your gun and let Jamie go."

"No!" Rocky shouted, and he volleyed wild-eyed glances from Jeb to her to Cullen. "I can't go to jail." He tapped the badge he still had clipped to the waist of his jeans. "You know what they do to cops in jail."

Jeb nodded. "I know, but you could be placed in solitary confinement—"

"I don't want to talk to you," Rocky interrupted, and this time the edges were even sharper. The man was losing it. "Leigh's the one who messed this up. She shouldn't be the sheriff. I should be."

But he stopped, and he didn't say anything else. She wondered if what he'd said had just sunk in. He was a killer, and there was no way he should be sheriff. He'd broken the very laws he'd sworn to uphold. Yes, the first—Alexa's murder—had no doubt been committed in the heat of the moment, but everything else since had been calculated.

So was what Leigh was about to do.

It was a risk, but she didn't want Rocky killing Jeb because he didn't want to hear what her father had to say. Leigh stepped out, took aim at Rocky.

"You have no right to wear that badge," she said, staring him right in the eyes.

With his gun trained on Rocky, Cullen stood, too, moving to Jeb's other side. Leigh wanted to yell at him for doing that. Especially since she figured that Rocky would indeed try to kill Cullen. But she knew he was feeling the same thing she was. Neither of them wanted the other to die. She could include Jeb in that, too.

"Don't you dare take a bullet for me," she snapped, aiming that at both Jeb and Cullen.

She might as well have been talking to the air though because she knew both of them would. Because they loved her.

Leigh stared at Rocky. "Put down your gun now."

Again, Rocky staggered back just a little, and Jamie made a strangled sound. Maybe because he thought this was all about to come to a head and that he'd die. And he might. Leigh couldn't make any guarantees that any of them would make it out of this alive.

"Do the right thing, Rocky," Jeb said.

Just as all hell broke loose.

The gunshot tore through the air. And also tore right into Rocky's leg. It took Leigh a moment to figure out where the shot had come from, but then she spotted Bowen. He was belly-down on the ground behind the truck, and he'd been the one to put another bullet in Rocky.

Rocky howled in pain, cursed and shoved Jamie forward. In the same motion, he brought up his gun.

Taking aim at Leigh.

Chapter Sixteen

Cullen didn't think. He just pulled the trigger, double-tapping it and sending two shots into Rocky's chest.

The moment seemed to freeze with the sound of the bullets echoing through the icy air. Rocky just stood there, his face masked with shock, and the blood already spreading across the front of his coat. Finally, he crumpled, dropping first to his knees before collapsing to the ground.

With Leigh right beside him, Cullen ran toward him. And behind them, he heard Jeb shout for the EMTs to come to the backyard. Rocky still had hold of his gun, and Cullen didn't want him having a chance to try to kill Leigh. They reached Rocky at the same time, and Leigh ripped the gun from his hand. She also frisked him for other weapons and found a backup gun and a knife in his boot holsters.

"Where's Cecile?" Leigh asked, aiming her question at Bowen.

"I used the ATV to take her to the ambulance. I left her with the EMTs while I came back to try to help."

Leigh released the breath she seemed to have been holding. "Thank you. You did help. Thank you for that, too."

Cullen doubted this would be the end of the bad blood between their families, but it was a good start. It was too bad that it'd nearly taken them all being killed before it happened.

Jamie pushed himself away from the truck and staggered toward Bowen, who caught him in his arms. "You okay?" Bowen asked him.

Jamie nodded, but Cullen thought the ranch hand was far from okay. He'd likely have to be admitted to the hospital again. But at least this time, there wouldn't be the threat of danger.

Well, maybe.

Rocky probably didn't have much time left. He was bleeding out fast, and even the EMTs likely wouldn't be able to keep him alive. That's why Cullen had to press him for answers now. If not, Leigh and Jamie might never have peace of mind.

Cullen got right in Rocky's face. "You said Alexa got herself killed? How?"

Clamming up, Rocky laid his head back on

the frozen ground and looked up at the sky. Leigh didn't stay quiet though. She read Rocky his rights. That was the smart thing to do in case Rocky survived.

"You really want to take all of this to the grave?" Cullen shrugged and shifted as if to get up. "Suit yourself. You'll be remembered for being an idiot and a coward."

"I'm neither of those things," Rocky snapped. He coughed, grimaced and then gathered his breath again. "Alexa got herself killed because she hated your guts. That's why. And she wanted me to help her set you up because she knew I could. She knew I was just that good." He was actually bragging now, puffing up his bloody chest. "Alexa was going to bruise up her face some and get me to say I'd witnessed you assaulting her."

Cullen felt his jaw tighten. Hell. If Alexa and Rocky had done that, it would have definitely caused him some trouble. Leigh might have had to arrest him after all. Especially with Alexa and Rocky pushing her to do just that.

"You were going to help Alexa frame Cullen?" Leigh demanded.

Rocky narrowed his eyes and gave her a defiant glare. "Yeah. But when I met her in Cullen's bathroom the night of the party, she said she'd changed her mind, that she was giving up on Cullen and wanted Austin instead."

Cullen gave that a moment to sink in. Yeah, he could see Alexa moving on to her next mark, and she might have enjoyed trying to twist up Austin and Kali.

"I told Alexa no, that I wasn't going to let you off the hook," Rocky snarled, and he aimed all that anger at Cullen. "I told her that if she didn't go through with it, then I'd go to Leigh and rat her out."

"I'm guessing Alexa didn't care much for that?" Leigh prompted.

"She didn't," Rocky verified in a snarl. "That's when Alexa called me, well, a lot of names. She shoved me, told me to get lost. Nobody talks to me that way. *Nobody.* I got the horse statue and bashed her on her idiot head."

Cullen could see all of that playing out. See it playing out with Jamie, too. He was betting that Alexa had mentioned Jamie bringing her to the Triple R. Rocky had probably wanted to make sure Alexa hadn't told Jamie that she was there to meet him. It would have been something similar with McNash. Rocky couldn't risk that Alexa had told the thug about her hiring Rocky.

And that left Kali and Austin.

With everything Rocky had just spelled out

for them, Cullen doubted Austin and Kali had had any part in the attacks. Austin had lied and cheated, and Kali had set up the ruse to get back at Austin, but if Rocky could have put some of this blame on them, he would have.

The EMTs came closer, but Rocky waved them off. "Nobody touches me. You think I want to live behind bars for the rest of my life? I don't," he said, answering his own question. He shifted his gaze to Leigh, who was staring down at him. "I want to say my piece. I want both of you to know how much I hate your guts."

The hatred was obvious, but it didn't enrage Cullen nearly as much as Rocky using that hatred to try to kill Leigh. He darn near succeeded, too. Any one of those fired shots could have left her dead.

"You're the one who called me," Jamie said. "Threatened me. You told me you'd kill me if I went to the cops."

Cullen glanced at his ranch hand, who was now being treated by the EMTs. Jamie was still plenty shaky. With good reason. He'd just come close to dying again. But there was some steel in Jamie's eyes, too. Ditto for Bowen's. His father moved away from Jamie to come closer to Rocky and them.

"So what if I threatened you?" Rocky

snapped, dismissing Jamie with a split-second glance. "I didn't want you remembering that I was the one who nearly bashed in your brains. I figured the calls would make you shut up."

"I didn't know it was you," Jamie fired back. "Not for sure, anyway. But I'd got to thinking that it could be you and that's why I wanted to talk to Leigh and Cullen after I got out of the hospital. I wouldn't have had any proof it was you if you hadn't kidnapped me."

"Oh, boo-hoo," Rocky taunted. "You whiner. Go home to your mommy."

"Oops," Bowen said, his voice dripping with sarcasm. He stepped on Rocky's leg. Right in the spot where Bowen had shot him minutes earlier.

Rocky gave a feral howl of pain. But nobody felt sorry for him. And nobody did anything to stop Bowen from adding even more pressure before he finally stepped back.

Leigh stooped down, and she waited until Rocky tore his narrowed gaze from Bowen and moved it back to her. "Who helped you with McNash's murder and the attacks against Cullen and me?" Leigh demanded. She didn't sound hateful or filled with anger. She sounded like a cop.

"Nobody," Rocky spat out. "I didn't need any help. I'm the one who fired those shots in the woods by Kali's house." He paused, winced and dragged in a ragged breath.

"Austin and Kali didn't work with you?" Leigh pressed.

Despite the obvious pain, Rocky managed a dry, nearly soundless laugh. "No, I didn't need them. Both of them are stupid. Austin was cheating with Alexa, and Kali was too blind to see what was right in front of her face. Alexa was a viper, ready to ruin anyone who got in her path." He looked at Cullen. "You were stupid, too, to ever get involved with her."

"It wasn't my finest moment," Cullen admitted. "But you've had some damn un-fine moments yourself. You wanted to kill Leigh because she beat you in the election. Because the majority of people in Dark River wanted her and not you for their sheriff. Considering what you've done, that was a seriously good decision on their part."

The light might have been dwindling from Rocky's eyes, but there was still plenty of bitterness and hatred in them. He looked past them at Jeb. "She shouldn't have the badge, Jeb. You shouldn't have the right to call her your daughter. She betrayed you with Cullen."

"*You* betrayed me," Jeb said, his voice hard and mean. "I'll be damned if you'll die wearing this." He reached down, tore off Rocky's badge and handed it to Leigh. "Now, go to hell, where you belong."

Jeb stepped back, letting the EMTs move in to start treating Rocky. Leigh stepped away, too, heading to Vance, who was making his way to them.

"How are Dawn and Cecile?" she immediately asked.

"They'll be okay. I had another ambulance come, and they're both on the way to the hospital."

Cullen knew Leigh would be checking on her deputies as soon as she could wrap up everything with Rocky. Leigh would also have to deal with some guilt for their injuries, and it wouldn't matter that it wasn't her fault. She'd still feel responsible that she hadn't been able to stop Rocky before he did so much damage.

"We also found a truck near Leigh's house," Vance added. "It's probably the vehicle Rocky used to get here." He glanced at Rocky. "He tried to kill you?"

Leigh nodded. "And he succeeded in killing Alexa and McNash. He just confessed."

Vance shook his head, muttered some profanity. "I'm sorry, Leigh," he said. "So sorry."

Cullen figured there was some guilt playing into that apology as well. Vance was a good cop, and he'd be kicking himself for not seeing that he'd been working with a dirty one.

"Is Rocky going to live?" Vance asked a moment later.

But the moment the question was out of his mouth, one of the EMTs stood and checked his watch. "Time of death is 9:35. You want me to go ahead and call the ME?"

She gave a weary nod, sighed and closed her eyes for a moment. Steadying herself. Cullen tried to help with that. He went to her, and despite the fact that they had an audience, he pulled her into his arms. Judging from the way she leaned into him, she needed the hug as much as he did.

While Vance dealt with the EMTs and the body, Cullen led Leigh up the back porch steps and into her kitchen. He left the door open though so they could still keep watch of what was going on.

"I'm not going to ask you if you're okay," Cullen whispered.

"Good. I won't ask you, either." But she did look up at him as if trying to see just how much this had shaken him.

He was shaken all right and could still hear the roar of the truck engine bearing down on them. But flashbacks and bad memories weren't going to overshadow the good feelings he had about Leigh. That was why he brushed a quick kiss over her mouth. It packed a punch despite being barely more than a peck.

"Should I have seen that Rocky was dirty?" she asked.

Cullen didn't even have to think about this. "No. Rocky hid the depth of his hatred. Well, until the end when he knew he was caught."

She stared at him, obviously considering that, and nodded. That nod was a victory and the start of her accepting that what Rocky had done was beyond her control.

Leigh moved out of the hug when Jeb came to the doorway, but she stayed close. Arm to arm with Cullen. And because they were still touching, he felt Leigh tense up a little. Probably because she didn't know what she was about to face with her father. Jeb obviously hadn't condoned Rocky's actions, but then, he might not condone her kissing Cullen, either.

"The town council won't have a leg to stand on if they try to dismiss you," Jeb said. His voice, like the rest of him, was coated in weariness. A man who'd seen way too much. Maybe there was some guilt, too, because he hadn't seen the dirty cop who'd worshiped him. "You held your ground and didn't arrest an innocent man."

"But I didn't arrest the guilty one before he could kill again," she muttered.

Jeb lifted his shoulder. "The town council, including me, gave Rocky the green light to go after you. We'll be eating that particular dish of crow for a while." He met her eye to eye. "Nobody's going to challenge you... Sheriff."

Leigh's arm tightened again when Jeb stuck out his hand for her to shake. It was hardly a tender family gesture, but coming from Jeb, it was practically a blessing of his support. Maybe his love, too.

Leigh shook his hand. Then relaxed. "Thank you. You taught me well."

Again, not especially tender, but Jeb blinked hard as if trying to keep his eyes dry. "What will you two do now?" he asked.

The timing was lousy, but Cullen decided to go ahead and declare his intentions. All of them. "I'm going to ask Leigh on a date. If she says yes, then I'll ask her on a second date. Then, a third. Then, a—"

"Yes," Leigh interrupted. And even though the timing was just as lousy for her, she smiled a little. "That's yes to the first, second and third."

"What about a fourth?" Cullen pressed.

She looked up at him. "Yes to that, too."

Cullen smiled as well, and he would have

kissed her long and hard if Jeb hadn't cleared his throat.

"I'll be going," Jeb muttered. He turned to leave, then stopped, his gaze going to Leigh's. "You probably don't want my opinion, but I think yes is the right answer. You should go on those dates with Cullen."

"She should," Bowen said.

Cullen hadn't realized his father was close enough to have heard their conversation, but obviously he had been.

"My son's in love with your daughter," Bowen added, sparing Jeb the briefest of glances.

Jeb nodded. "And she's in love with him." He lifted his hand in farewell and walked away.

Leigh stood there. Her eyes wide. Her body still.

"You look stunned," Cullen said.

"I am," she admitted.

"Because you didn't know you were in love with me?" Cullen clarified, sliding his arm back around her.

"No, because our fathers didn't take swipes at each other." She looked up at him. "I'd already figured out I was in love with you."

Now Cullen did kiss her, and he didn't give a rat that his father and everybody else was watching.

"I know you're about to get busy with reports and such, but I'll want to hear more about how you figured out you were in love with me," he said with his mouth against hers.

"We can get into that on our fifth date," Leigh whispered, and she kissed him right back.

* * * * *

Look for more books in USA TODAY *bestselling author Delores Fossen's miniseries,*
The Law in Lubbock County,
when Maverick Justice
goes on sale next month, only from
Harlequin Intrigue!

Get 4 FREE REWARDS!

We'll send you 2 FREE Books plus 2 FREE Mystery Gifts.

FREE Value Over **$20**

Both the **Worldwide Library** and **Essential Suspense** series feature compelling novels filled with gripping mysteries, edge of your seat thrillers and heart-stopping romantic suspense stories.

YES! Please send me 2 FREE novels from the Worldwide Library or Essential Suspense Collection and my 2 FREE gifts (gifts are worth about $10 retail). After receiving them, if I don't wish to receive any more books, I can return the shipping statement marked "cancel." If I don't cancel, I will receive 4 brand-new Worldwide Library books every month and be billed just $6.24 each in the U.S. or $6.74 each in Canada, a savings of at least 22% off the cover price or 4 brand-new Essential Suspense books every month and be billed just $7.24 each in the U.S. or $7.49 each in Canada, a savings of at least 28% off the cover price. It's quite a bargain! Shipping and handling is just 50¢ per book in the U.S. and $1.25 per book in Canada.* I understand that accepting the 2 free books and gifts places me under no obligation to buy anything. I can always return a shipment and cancel at any time. The free books and gifts are mine to keep no matter what I decide.

Choose one: ☐ **Worldwide Library**
(414/424 WDN GNNZ)

☐ **Essential Suspense**
(191/391 MDN GNNZ)

Name (please print)

Address   Apt. #

City   State/Province   Zip/Postal Code

Email: Please check this box ☐ if you would like to receive newsletters and promotional emails from Harlequin Enterprises ULC and its affiliates. You can unsubscribe anytime.

Mail to the Harlequin Reader Service:
IN U.S.A.: P.O. Box 1341, Buffalo, NY 14240-8531
IN CANADA: P.O. Box 603, Fort Erie, Ontario L2A 5X3

Want to try 2 free books from another series! Call 1-800-873-8635 or visit www.ReaderService.com.

*Terms and prices subject to change without notice. Prices do not include sales taxes, which will be charged (if applicable) based on your state or country of residence. Canadian residents will be charged applicable taxes. Offer not valid in Quebec. This offer is limited to one order per household. Books received may not be as shown. Not valid for current subscribers to the Worldwide Library or Essential Suspense Collection. All orders subject to approval. Credit or debit balances in a customer's account(s) may be offset by any other outstanding balance owed by or to the customer. Please allow 4 to 6 weeks for delivery. Offer available while quantities last.

Your Privacy—Your information is being collected by Harlequin Enterprises ULC, operating as Harlequin Reader Service. For a complete summary of the information we collect, how we use this information and to whom it is disclosed, please visit our privacy notice located at corporate.harlequin.com/privacy-notice. From time to time we may also exchange your personal information with reputable third parties. If you wish to opt out of this sharing of your personal information, please visit readerservice.com/consumerschoice or call 1-800-873-8635. **Notice to California Residents**—Under California law, you have specific rights to control and access your data. For more information on these rights and how to exercise them, visit corporate.harlequin.com/california-privacy.

WWLSTSUS22